Lucy's Eggs

Lucy's Eggs

Short Stories and a Novella

• • •

RICK HENRY

Syracuse University Press

06   07   08   09   10   11   6   5   4   3   2   1

Several stories in this volume were previously published in literary
reviews: "Having Airs" in the 1996 issue of *Short Story*;
"Muttering Something about Raising Cain" in the 2000 issue of the
Vermont Literary Review; and "The Telephone Girl" in the
Fall 2005 issue of the *Connecticut Review*.

The quotation by Edward Sapir appearing in "The Telephone Girl" is
taken from his 1924 essay, "Culture, Genuine and Spurious."

The paper used in this publication meets the minimum requirements of American
National Standard of Information Sciences—Permanence of
Paper of Printed Library Materials, ANSI Z39.48–1984©™

Library of Congress Cataloging-in-Publication Data
Henry, Richard.
Lucy's eggs : short stories and a novella / Rick Henry.—1st ed.
p. cm.
ISBN 0–8156–0850–0 (alk. paper)
1. Homer (N.Y.)—Fiction. I. Title.
PS3608.E579L83 2006
813'.6—dc22   2006008451

Manufactured in the United States of America

For S, as always

Rick Henry teaches literature, linguistics, and writing and has published fiction and articles in a variety of journals and anthologies. *Pretending and Meaning: Toward a Pragmatic Theory of Fictional Discourse,* a philosophical inquiry into the pragmatic foundations of fictional discourse, was published by Greenwood Publishing (1996). *Sidewalk Portrait: Fifty-fourth Floor and Falling,* a novella, was published by BlazeVox Books (2006). Henry is coeditor of *The Blueline Anthology* (Syracuse University Press, 2004). He is currently an associate professor of English at SUNY-Potsdam and editor of *Blueline.*

• • •

Contents

Lucy's Eggs

· · ·

Having Airs

EUNICE HAD AIRS. Or so said her Aunt Mabeline at the wedding. Eunice didn't quite understand. "You mean like Uncle Joe has airs?" Her Aunt Mabeline turned red in the face, either from laughter or embarrassment. "No child, that's wind. Your Uncle Joe's got wind. You got airs."

Everyone was crackling over Mabeline's cooking so Eunice sat quiet, thinking, her hands folded in her lap the way her mother taught her, like a butterfly at rest. She was glad, at least, for not having Uncle Joe's wind. Having his nose was bad enough. Her Aunt Katherine said noses were like blessings—so special they usually skipped a generation. "Bequeathed upon one's heirs" was the precise way her Aunt Katherine put it, punctuating herself with an upward jut of her nose that meant it was a family thing. Aunt Katherine did that a lot ("Juting," said her Uncle Joe dragging out the ooo, "because being Anglo-Saxon isn't good enough for her"), which only meant there were a lot of family things to keep track of. Eunice had asked her grandfather who his heirs were. He'd scoffed. "Heirs? What'd I want with heirs? The only thing I got worth anything is your grandmother—and who'd take her?" Eunice didn't tell him she'd be happy to inherit her grandmother. If she could trade her grandmother for her uncle's nose, she'd take her grandmother every day. She drew in her breath and exhaled, her hands, her butterfly wings fluttering to settle again in her lap. First her nose, then her airs. Eunice wasn't sure she wanted to be so special.

The laughter was just settling to a comfortable and occasional chuckle when her Uncle Joe stepped from the kitchen to the porch. Just the sight of him set it off again. Their laughter lifted the night when they saw he was carrying a double helping of Mabeline's beans. "Island beans" she called them, a recipe she created when they were in San Juan. They were nasty beans, little black rocks all smothered with sour cream and enough lime to wrinkle wood. Uncle Joe was the only one who ever ate them, though Aunt Mabeline didn't know. He didn't want her feelings hurt so he saw that the bowl his wife brought to family get-togethers always went home empty. And that didn't mean slipping it to the dogs, nor burying it under a tree.

Eunice thought she knew what "airs" were without asking, but she went in search of her grandfather's dictionary. On the way, she had an air just as plain as everyone sitting on the porch watching Uncle Joe spooning in those beans. Maybe it was the beans, or her turning her back on them, but everything got very close, very thick, and she started to sweat. Her Aunt Mabeline's voice felt like it was coming from inside her head, lurking in the corners, filling out the spaces with the roundness and depth of her laughter. Mabeline was telling everyone about the dances at the Air Force base on San Juan; Eunice could see her talking just like it was happening right then, though of course she was only remembering what Mabeline said yesterday in the kitchen, or rather, what Mabeline would have really said in the kitchen yesterday if it wasn't really just part of her airs. That was the tricky part sometimes—getting it right. Did Aunt Mabeline really talk about the Air Force base yesterday or didn't she? Remembering that her aunt and uncle only arrived this morning helped, but it wasn't always so easy. And the airs were usually all so real. Aunt Mabeline was telling everyone about San Juan, about the Air

Force base and entertaining the pilots and mechanics. All the while she was scraping the skins off apples—just to be a bit of help to Grandma, seeing how Grandma was going to make her world famous apple pie for the wedding. Grandma was rolling her eyes, but you couldn't tell whether it was from the way Aunt Mabeline was peeling the apples, or because Aunt Mabeline was an "entertainer," as Grandma put it. Grandpa didn't care one way or the other. He was just hovering around because once word got out that Grandma was making her apple pies, all of Homer would be rushing up the drive.

Apples. Eunice felt the word for a moment, a hesitant attention to the sound of it. Of course she knew better. Even the slightest glance, the tiniest bit of attention, brought a kind of vertigo. Her Aunt Mabeline's voice faded to an incessant murmur, the sound of a bushel of apples spilling down the porch steps. Eunice gripped the rail all the more tightly until it passed. Then the night air smelled fresh, clean, the way it feels after a thunderstorm, that burning electric clean that lightning produces. She felt a chill, took a deep breath to clear her head, and skipped off to find the dictionary.

"Imagine," said her Aunt Mabeline as Eunice hit the bottom step, "a dozen sailors tumbling head over heels down the gangplank!" That set them all laughing again.

$\bullet \quad \bullet \quad \bullet$

"Grandpa," Eunice asked the next day. "Do you think my nose is stuck?"

They were in the orchard. Twelve acres of apples Eunice's grandfather had planted over twenty years ago. They were Romes, in case a stranger asked, the local variety everyone grew. What else would they be? Considering the claims Homerians made to Romes in particular and apples in general, visitors to the region might think they'd arrived in Eden, site of The Very First Apple.

Residents took some pride in thoughts of such Biblical proportions, swelling their chests with the fresh and fragrant air and swaggering about the orchards; roadside stands reenacted medieval morality plays with every purchase. Visitors were accosted by these modern-day tempters who were ready to cut a slice of any apple on the table for a taste. The knowledge engendered in the touch of tongue to just one of those apples! Taste buds awakened, no, not just awakened, sprung to life itself! Never again would the unwary be satisfied with just any apple from the grocer. There isn't a child in the area that hasn't been called (affectionately of course) a little devil.

"Do you think my nose is stuck?" Eunice had to ask again.

She held the stepladder her grandfather stood upon. It shook with his weight and the constant shifting of his feet as he stretched for the apples just out of arm's reach. She had offered to climb the tree, but he had set his jaw and pulled the ladder from the back of the truck. It wiggled so much she could barely hold on. She could hear him grunting from the strain. She didn't know he ever grunted and wondered if it was something her Aunt Katherine would jute about. Her Uncle Joe grunted all the time. She had been worried about that, grunting. She had supposed grunts would, like noses, skip a generation; but how could she tell? She might just be special enough to get her uncle's nose *and* his grunts—unless grunts were more like wind. And where did airs fit? Aunt Mabeline said her uncle grunted because he had a deviated septum. Her grandmother huffed at that. "I didn't raise no deviant," she said, genuinely angry. But Mabeline just laughed like she always did, making Grandma even madder. Her grandmother didn't like it when Aunt Mabeline laughed. Her grandmother didn't like Aunt Mabeline—period. A family thing, nodded her Aunt Katherine, something to do with the inheritance. It seems Grandma had a whole lot of things more valuable than Grandpa.

"It means his nose is blocked," said Mabeline, "he can't always get his air."

"What?" said her grandfather. An apple fell to the ground.

"Do you think my nose is stuck?" she asked for the third time.

"Stuck?" he repeated. "Of course I'm not stuck."

"No," she called up to him. "My nose!"

"I shouldn't worry about your nose," he said. "Is the most stunning nose in the whole county. Is the perfect Anfall nose. It will smell out the perfect boyfriend soon? They always do."

Eunice began to really worry about her nose. Everyone was worried about her nose. What was wrong with it? Was it connected to her airs? The ladder shook a little more and her grandfather's foot almost kicked her right in her worry spot.

"Eunice?"

"Yes Grandpa?"

"You run as fast as you can and get your Uncle Joe. Don't say a word to your grandmother, just get your Uncle Joe, you hear?"

•   •   •

Eunice ran as fast as she could to get her Uncle Joe. She ran faster than she thought she could, and faster than her Uncle Joe on the way back through the trees. There were hundreds of them, trees that is, or so it seemed, hundreds of trees whizzing by as she ran, her legs pumping up and down, her breathing shorter and shorter until she couldn't breathe anymore. Her uncle passed her as they got to her grandfather. His legs were still dangling; she could see them against the leaves, flopping about the air. "Hoist-jerking" her Aunt Mabeline would have said, if she were there to say anything at all. But Eunice heard her Aunt Mabeline plain as plain-speaking, as plain as the nose on her face, telling everyone to get him down before he hoist-jerked himself right out of the tree and onto his head. Grandpa was dangling. The ladder was on its side in the grass.

Eunice was out of breath. Grandpa holding on, grunting, the ladder just as still as still is. She couldn't catch her breath with those legs hanging there the way they were, with the grass so long and tall, with the wind picking up so that his legs and the grass— over eight kinds of grass with eight different colors her father had shown her—were waving in time to each other, with Uncle Joe and her grandfather grunting together, a sound that separated itself from the wind and engulfed her just as a gust swirled up and sent her hair flying about with the grass.

·   ·   ·

"It was a succubus," said Aunt Mabeline.

"A what?" said Aunt Katherine.

"She ought to watch her mouth," said Grandma, wiping dishes and talking to their shine. Grandma never looked at Aunt Mabeline. One look was more than she'd ever need, she'd said more than once.

"A succubus," repeated Aunt Mabeline. "They live in trees, sometimes fruit trees, sometimes nut trees, any kind I suppose. They're spirits that try to capture men."

"How does she know these things?" said Aunt Katherine. "It isn't natural to know such things."

"And you," said Grandma, turning to Grandpa. "You best stay out of those trees. I'm not warning you twice." Grandma didn't really believe Mabeline, not really. But she wasn't willing to take a chance.

Grandpa almost liked the idea of getting himself captured by a tree spirit, but he had his face on tight so Grandma wouldn't get the wrong idea.

·   ·   ·

"Stuck-up, stuck-up, Eunice is a stuck-up." Eunice's younger cousins were racing about the apple stand. She wished she hadn't said anything when they came around again, tagging her and run-

ning away. "You're it! You're it! Stuck-up! Stuck-up! Eunice is it!"
The little brats might get a surprise yet when their noses started
growing. Eunice lunged for the nearest one. He shrieked and ran
into the table, toppling it. Twenty bushels of apples spilled and
rolled over the ground.

"Ach! Out! You little demons!" growled her grandfather. "Eunice, pick up those apples."

An older woman with out-of-state plates on her car was asking
about the difference between these apples and the ones they were
selling a few miles down the road in Cortland.

"Are these baking apples?" she asked. "Can you eat them?"

The mere mention of Cortland was enough to set Eunice's
grandfather off, a sight to see, a sight all of Homer would pay good
money to see, a sight they'd talk about all the way to Virgil, but
Eunice was too busy fighting off another of her airs. The apples
rolling about the grass, her cousins yelling over and over about
her nose, the woman whinnying "Cortland Cortland," a nasal
horsey whine rising to a shriek, the apples tumbling down the
porch steps, her Aunt Mabeline murmuring something about
customers pawing over the golden apples of the Hesperides. . . .

·   ·   ·

"Should get her to a doctor," said one of the neighbors, chewing
on the stub end of an ear of corn. "It ain't natural for a child to be
jumping and jigging like that."

"Possessed by the devil!" said the woman with out-of-state
plates.

"Just hush," said Aunt Katherine, "you'll scare the girl. Besides, she's all better now, aren't you, honey."

Eunice didn't feel better, she never did. A little thirsty, but not
better. It didn't help to have all these faces staring at her.

"You can't do that," said Aunt Katherine. "You scare us half to
death, your going away like that."

"A visitation," said the woman with out-of-state plates. "The devil's behind this, you'll see." She was backing away, afraid to turn her back to the small crowd gathered around Eunice.

"Could I have a glass of water?" asked Eunice.

Uncle Joe came muscling in through the faces.

"Give her some air," he said. "What you want to do, suffocate the girl?"

"Suffocate? With that nose?" said another customer.

Eunice didn't want any more air. She was sick to death of air. She was sick to death of being special.

"How are you feeling, dear?" asked her Aunt Mabeline. She was reaching in, pushing a glass of water toward her, and giving her Uncle Joe a good nudge on her way by. "Let's get you up to the house now."

•   •   •

Eunice was lying on the hammock on the porch, in her grandfather's special hammock that he never let anyone use. She could hear them in the kitchen talking away while her grandmother cooked. She was making another apple pie. Eunice could tell by the way the knife sounded against the board.

"Maybe it was one of them succubuses," said her grandmother.

"I dropped him pretty good, didn't I?" said her Uncle Joe.

"Incubus," said Aunt Mabeline. "That's incubus, women are attacked by incubi, men by succubi."

"But she's just a child!" said her Aunt Katherine.

"Like I said, that isn't natural, her jumping all about over the ground."

"Like she was dancing to that new sex music."

"Sucked up by an incubus."

"Dancing, sex . . ."

"Watch your mouth."

"Decked him good. Last time he'll make a crack about an Anfall nose."

"It means another wedding's coming," said her Aunt Mabeline.

"How does she know these things?" said her grandmother, sounding just like her Aunt Katherine. "It isn't natural to know such things." Her knife hit the board hard.

"We'll let her sleep out there." Her Aunt Katherine's voice. "The air will do her good."

·   ·   ·

It is dark. Eunice wakes suddenly. She isn't in her grandfather's hammock. She hears clapping in the night. Her eyes adjust to the blackness, to the guest room at her grandfather's house. The sheets smell fresh, her grandmother's prized possession—a closet full of linen. The clapping stops. Eunice can see their hands returning to their laps, butterflies resting for the night. Her Aunt Mabeline thanks everyone. "I'd like to sing an old lay, a eighteenth century air." She can hear her Uncle Joe strumming the guitar on the porch below the window, and her Aunt Mabeline clear her throat.

> There is in souls a sympathy with sounds;
> And, as the mind is pitch'd the ear is pleased
> With melting airs, or martial, brisk, or grave. . . .

Her aunt's voice rises rich and melodious through the summer night, caught on the wings of the fireflies. Eunice listens to the sounds, the fullness of her aunt's voice working into the innermost recesses of her mind, holding court, filling the tiniest of spaces, melting resistance, her mind floating with the fireflies before suddenly and slightly pitching to the steady drumming of apples tumbling across the porch, a knight bending to pick one up for his damsel. . . . She tries to look away, to close her eyes in the night against the murmuring, the knights, their armor glittering, the damsels in such bright colors. "Don't look," she whispers in the dark. "Don't look." But the colors are lovely, the dresses everyone is wearing, and the knights, so handsome. . . .

· · ·

The Cardinal Wars

"THEY ALL RISE UP AT ONCE in a fluttering burst of yellow, and then, whoosh, they vanish for the winter."

Lily's hands jerked and spasmed upward in a dramatic recreation, and then came swiftly down again, press thump press thump press thump with a mechanical certainty.

"They're due February 16th." She handed the three books to Marianne Chambers, who slipped them into her open bag.

"I've heard cardinals do the same thing." Marianne nodded and set her lips as she said it, gestures calculated to enhance her authority. Marianne was one of the grand dames of the town. She had taken to wearing red. She fluffed her hair every few moments.

El wanted to say "nonsense." She wanted to burst in, set things straight. It was the fourth time she'd heard Lily acting out The Flight of the Goldfinches; goldfinches did not vanish for the winter. They lost their colors, but they did not vanish. As for the cardinals, it was better not to comment. Marianne lived across the road from El. Even though Marianne's house was set back from the busy highway, it was difficult not to see the splashes of red fluttering about. Especially after hearing their distinctive *sweet sweet sweet sweet.*

El turned away from the women and pushed the cart into the stacks, where she began reshelving the books. The process was vaguely bird-like: she'd shuffle to the side, tilt her head, and peck

11

at the shelf with her hand. El shoved that image aside. She liked birds. She did not want to be bird-like.

•   •   •

"You know winter's here," said Lily to a young woman. A toddler clung to the woman, hiding behind her legs. El was just returning from lunch. The door banged behind her. The toddler burst into a wail in the middle of Lily's performance: ". . . and then, whoosh, they vanish for the winter." The performance was calculated for the toddler's benefit. It had built to the "whoosh," a whoosh accompanied by wide eyes and a bit of extra flittering of Lily's hands. Her fingernails, red and pointed, scratched the air.

"There now," Lily cooed, press thump press thump press thump press thump press thump. "Don't worry. They'll be back in the spring."

El disappeared into the stacks again, pretending she was walking through the woods in summer, into the QLs for a book on cardinals. In the soft light, it was difficult to pretend. The light drained the colors from the spines and they all seemed to fade to a muted mix, hardly the woods, hardly the vibrant greens. Hardly the lively smells on the wind. Instead, must and dust. She was pretending, badly, that she was walking through the woods in summer, listening for the sweet sounds of cardinals. There wasn't one. All of the books on birds were checked out. Press thump press thump press thump.

•   •   •

For the next week, the clouds pressed low against the snow, gray pressing into the white, drear into dreary. El couldn't say why, exactly, but she needed to see the cardinals. She needed the dash of red against the gray and white and brown outside her window. Gray and white and brown and white and gray and white and brown and gray . . . it seemed as though it would never end. It seemed as though January would never end. *She* would like to rise in a sudden burst, whoosh, and then vanish for the rest of the winter. *She* would like to head south, for the colors more than the warmth. Instead, she slid into her overcoat and headed to the feed store. Her coat was ochre, at least that's what her coat matched against the color wheel in the paint department as she wandered on past. When she bought it, years ago, it was bright yellow. She tried not to think that it was slowly fading to brown. Gray and white and brown.

She returned with two bird feeders and a fifty-pound bag of birdseed. They were safflower seeds, precracked for the white nut inside. Perfect, her mother had told her over the telephone from Florida, the land where the goldfinches held their colors year-round. Perfect for the cardinals, her mother had told her on Sunday. We used to feed the cardinals in the winter, when you were a baby. Remember? Just talking to her mother was brown and white and gray. El considered, for a fleeting moment, not calling her the following Sunday.

It took nothing to hang the feeders in the apple tree. Nothing to fill them. She returned to her window for a few moments, but only for a few moments. It would take a while for the birds, for the cardinals, to find the seed. She burrowed into her closet, looking for a box of socks, an old box that had red socks and blue socks and green socks. El needed colors, and she needed them badly.

Later, after lunch, she pressed against the window, fogging it with her breath, and settling back just a bit. She had a view of the west, a sloping hill, with fields in the background and lines of trees and low scrub between them, property markers. The sunsets were spectacular, when she got them. In January, she got clouds. Gray against the white snow and the browns of the fields poking through. Drear against the dreary.

It had begun to snow. Lightly. Nothing that would accumulate, but land and sky became one. She saw amidst the swirling flakes that the chickadees had found the feeder. They were busy, a small flock of black and white flinging seed to the ground, flitting from the feeders to the branches to the ground and back. The motion was chaotic and soothing, like the swirling snow itself. She sat on her sofa, tea steaming lightly on the table, and her box of socks at her feet. They were summer weight. Wholly inappropriate for January. But they were comforting, tightly packed balls of color. A squirrel hopped along a horizontal branch, found the feeder, and hung, upside down, scattering more seed on the ground. The chickadees barely flit a wing.

Later that afternoon, she stepped outside for a breath of fresh air. It was growing colder. The radio was calling for a wind chill advisory—thirty to forty degrees below zero. For the moment all was calm. The snow had stopped long ago. Across the road, to the north, deep in the bushes that surrounded the Chambers's house and hid it from the road, she heard the *sweet sweet sweet sweet* of a cardinal. In one short breath, she could feel her nose growing red in the chill, and she stepped back inside.

By Sunday afternoon, the chickadees and squirrel had been joined by a burst of goldfinches in their winter drab, a handful of blue jays, and two chipmunks. The goldfinches swooped in. The chickadees flittered out. El shivered. Even the blue of the jays was not enough against the gray skies. The phone rang and her hand hovered over the receiver. Two rings. Three. She picked it up, caught by her mother, caught by thoughts of green golf courses and the bright shimmering of sun off blue-windowed buildings and red convertibles humming about, their tops fluffing in the bright southern light. El almost, almost, preferred the drear against the dreary. Would prefer it, if she had a splash of red and could hear the *sweet sweet sweet sweet*.

•　　•　　•

The week passed, slowly, claustrophobically. The temperatures slid, downward, below zero, below ten below zero with the threat of a colder air mass to follow. The world was sharp and harsh. Tires crunched and whined; aching engines pierced the air. On Monday, the library was closed. On Tuesday, closed because of the cold. On Wednesday, only a handful of children arrived for story hour. El had discovered deep in the children's section, *Sweet Sweet, How Sweet is My Baby?* She read with great animation as baby bears and rhinoceroses and kittens and puppies learned to walk and run and play. She growled and grumbled and meowed and barked with the babies. She surprised herself when she turned a page and found a baby cardinal breaking out of its shell in a nest. Its mother fed and fed the baby until it was big enough to fly. And whoosh, the baby and its mother flew up into the sky in brilliant red flashes. She almost opened her arms like wings and called *sweet sweet sweet sweet* as they soared. One of the young boys in the back said "and whoosh, they vanish for the winter and fly all the way to Florida!" He jerked and spasmed and fluttered his hands. The rest of the children clapped and laughed.

Later in the afternoon, after her story hour, after bundling up the children in their brightly colored hats and scarves and mittens and gloves, she returned home. In the driveway, behind the slowly fogging glass of her windshield, she caught a glimpse—a flash of red as a male cardinal inspected her feeders. He hopped along the apple branch. A jay dropped, a blue bomb, landing on the snow. He cawed three times and rose, leaving a fan in the powder—impressions of his feathers pressed into the white. The cardinal hopped closer. Chickadees flitted about. El willed the cardinal to the feeder, one hop at a time. One hop at a time, it hopped closer, seemingly unaware of the distractions of the other birds. The cardinal was a bold gash of red in the tree. El drank in its color, felt its warmth inside her chest, radiant, radiating.

The cardinal landed on the feeder. He pulled out a few seeds, one at a time, tested them with a harsh crack against the wood, and flew off, across the road to Marianne's.

El sat in the loneliness left behind as the afternoon faded into evening and the car grew colder.

• • •

On Fridays, El ate lunch in the bagel shop. She treated herself to a specialty coffee. The cup warmed her hands. Whiffs of steam rose lazily. The walk from the library wasn't more than a block, but even at that short distance, the cold crept through the layers of her clothing to give her a serious chill. She spotted Marianne in the corner by the window, head bent in conspiratorial conversation with Jack Williston. Marianne's fingers twitched as she tried to fluff her hair with her head bent close to Jack's. El overheard talk about a heated birdbath, but she could not catch the substance. Her sandwich arrived, wilted, brown lettuce on a brown bagel. She chewed slowly. Winter would pass, she told herself. It had before.

Lunch passed. Her return walk to the library—cold. Her afternoon—drear. Her short drive home—cold and drear. As she got out of her car at the road to check her mail, a light gray car, encrusted with the salt and sludge that the highway department spread over the roads, accelerated, its driver pressing his foot to the floor now that she was out of his way, and he raced by, thumping a bass note, an ominous streak against the white and brown road. As its engine faded, she could hear a flurry of wings from the Chambers's and competing *sweet sweet sweet sweets* from no fewer than four male cardinals.

It was a wonder she hadn't lost the chickadees to the heated bath across the way. But the chickadees continued to flit about, rising en masse at the surprise arrival of a squirrel. Black and white. Black and white. She sat on her sofa, the summer socks at her sides, a comfort. The streak of blue outside barely attracted her attention—but the chickadees swirled up again, too late, and the jay cried victory: it had a chickadee pressed into the snow and it pecked, leisurely pulling feathers off the small bird, pausing to crow his triumph. El leapt from her sofa and bolted through her door to save the chickadee, but the jay merely flew up and away, across the road, toward Marianne's, the now limp chickadee in its beak. A dead chickadee for Marianne.

The clouds grew brighter. They dimmed to black. Brighter and dimmed to black. Brighter and dimmed to black. The days faded into nights; the nights faded into days. Lily told her story again, this time to a group of opened-mouthed five-year-olds. She had been revising, noted El. Now the goldfinches were absorbing all of the light from the sun so that they had enough energy to make it to the South. "That's why it gets so cloudy," she said, "and then they all rise up at once in a fluttering burst of yellow, and then, whoosh, they vanish for the winter." Her hands jerked and spasmed upward in a dramatic recreation that had yet to be revised. One little girl in a brown and white jumper pouted. "I hate goldfinches," she said. "I hate them."

Two weeks dragged by, minute by minute. El buried herself in the stacks, away from the windows, away from the drear. She checked the shelves for the bird books again, just as she had every morning and every afternoon for the past two weeks. They were still on loan. She checked the catalogue just as she had every morning and every afternoon. Marianne had them all. She tried not to curse. It was a library, sacred second only to a church. She allowed herself a whispered "damn." It wasn't the curse that was bad in the library, she decided, it was the volume. She allowed herself another whispered "damn." It was a far cry from the *sweet sweet sweet sweet* she needed so badly.

•   •   •

The feed store always had the comforting smell of grain dust and cat urine. It wasn't very big, three short aisles with a few bird feeders, garden gloves, some rakes, shovels and hoes, and the paint. Mostly covered with grain dust as they awaited spring with a patience greater than El's. Most of the feed, grain, and other stock was in the back. Still, she walked these aisles as she always walked them, without really seeing anything, just soaking up the smells. They almost smelled reassuring compared to the stark and frozen winter air outside. They almost smelled like colors. A couple of bird baths leaned against one wall. One circulated water during the summer. It spurted out of a clay frog's mouth. The tag said it had a heater in it, too. For the coldest of days. The tag also told her it would cost her a week's salary.

Jim, behind the counter, was on the phone. El traced her finger in the dust, thought about signing her name, thought about goldfinches, thought about losing her colors in a rising swirl as she flew south for the winter. Press thump. Her face was red. She could feel it burning in the warmth of the store as she waited for Jim to hang up. She needed salt for the softener. She was a week late, maybe two, refilling the tank. She could feel the hard water against her skin as she showered, as she washed her face in the morning. Foolish, really. Winter was hard enough without hard water.

Her ears tingled. Jim was recommending sunflowers for cardinals, but only the black oily kind. "The others aren't worth a *damn.*" In the feed store, you could swear and do it as loud as you liked.

El added a fifty-pound bag to her order for the salt.

"You're lucky," said Jim. "It's the last bag. Your neighbor was in a while back and bought ten bags. Can you imagine five hundred pounds of sunflower seeds?"

•　　•　　•

Three days later, El woke to the *sweet sweet sweet sweet* of the male, two males, calling their mates. She dashed to her window. Just on her side of the road, in a cedar, sat one of the males. His comb danced on the top of his head as he *sweet*ed. His red was a godsend. His *sweet sweet sweet sweet* was a godsend. Two cedars down, the splash of another male. Another comb dancing. Another *sweet sweet sweet sweet*. They surveyed her yard. They surveyed her feeder from the cedars, the black, oily sunflowers barely visible to El under the mass of chickadees and brown goldfinches.

The males *sweet sweet sweet sweet*ed and dared to move closer. One landed on the apple. Another on the ground maybe twenty feet from the feeder. A blue jay dropped down on the chickadees, scattering them in a rush, swirling up, brown against the gray sky. Press thump, smiled El, uttered sotto voce, like a curse in the library. Another jay landed, a foot or two from the cardinal on the ground. The cardinal barely ruffled a feather. Barely ceased its *sweet sweet sweet sweet*. For a moment, El thought the two males were competing, calling for the same female. She scanned the cedars; the females would follow, more cautiously, their muted colors were year-round, to protect them from the world. The males were more brazen. Louder. More. Just more. El squeezed herself with her good luck. She positively absorbed the colors. Absorbed their song. One male, the one in the apple, swooped down to the ground underneath the feeder. The chickadees had been busy scattering the seeds. The cardinal took one and flew back to the apple. He tested it, snapping with precision on the oily black of the outer hull. The other male hopped over and grasped another seed, cracked it without leaving. And another.

Their *sweet sweet sweet sweet*s suddenly fell away as they filled their beaks with the oily seeds. El watched them with half an eye, unable to exhale, unable to fog the window with her breath. She watched the cedars more carefully for the females. If they came, if they settled in, she could breathe. She could breathe.

It took some time. The goldfinches swirled up and away south a dozen times, two dozen times. The blue jays scattered the chickadees up and away. Up and away. The males paused every so often, to call to their mates, but only so often. They ate, storing up for the night. Or for Lily's newest story about cardinals swirling up into the sun each fall. Press thump. Press thump. El felt the beat of her heart as they ate. Press thump. Her heart was squeezed with the excitement.

And suddenly, a female. In one of the cedars. Ruffling her feathers.

And just as suddenly, she exhaled, a long breath, a life-giving breath.

The phone rang and drew her attention from the female. The clock let her know how late she was. The head librarian did as well. El claimed a cold. Flu-like symptoms. No sense infecting the children at story hour.

When she turned her attention to the feeder, she saw all four females on the ground working their way through the seeds. Their mates had stopped eating and were surveying the yard for danger. They called "all clear" over and over and over again with their steady song. El couldn't tear herself away from the window to eat. She simply sat, hugging her knees to her chest for the next three hours as the females fluttered from the ground to the cedars to the ground, as the males ruffled and fluffed and sang.

•   •   •

Every Thursday, El processed overdue notices at a small desk with a partial view of the door. In the winter, she also received a partial draft every time the door swung open and shut. Story hour was much more fun. So was reshelving books. Thursdays, however, meant pulling cards from the file, matching each card with a name and an address, copying out the address and the title of the book on a slip of paper that went into an envelope. Then, she had to take the stack of file cards, and one by one stamp them with red ink—OVERDUE. Press thump press thump press thump. The door swung open. A below-zero whoosh ran across the floor and sent chills up her legs. She heard Marianne's nattering even before the cold touched her boots. El peeked around the corner at her neighbor, whose arms were filled with books.

"I need to renew these," she said to Lily, who was poised, a statue ready for animation. Even after weeks of performances, she was more than ready to recreate her goldfinch drama. An extended run, held over by popular demand. El ducked back behind the column that hid her from the front desk. Press thump press thump press thump. The thumps were strangely satisfying.

Lily picked up one of the books. A bird book.

"Jack Williston was in yesterday. He said you had a regular bird sanctuary up there on the hill." Lily smiled. Glanced at another bird book.

"Oh Jack," Marianne smiled, her hand rose to fluff her hair. "Hardly a sanctuary. The cardinals seem to like it. I don't know why. There must be thirty or forty of them raising a racket up there. I must have a green thumb for them."

El tried not to cough. Eight. There were eight cardinals easing the winter with their singing.

"Returns?" asked Lily as she collected the pile of books from Marianne. "It hardly seems like you need them."

"Renews," said Marianne. "I'm still trying to figure out what's so special about my yard. You really should stop by, it is a sight to see them all over the trees. It's like they're announcing the end of the world."

Press THUMP. El stamped OVERDUE on the cards for Marianne's bird books and set them aside.

Lily came back with her own cold chill and pulled Marianne's notices from the pile.

"You're lucky," she said to Marianne, as she returned to the front desk. "We were just ready to send out the overdue notices."

Press thump press thump press thump. Lily renewed Marianne's books in half a minute and tossed the cards into the box for El to process after she was done with the overdue notices. El held her breath, hoping for a quick and timely whoosh of icy air as Marianne left the library. It didn't come soon enough. El felt herself turning blue.

•   •   •

The cardinals disappeared again, back across the road to Marianne's. She could hear their *sweet sweet sweet sweet*s through the trees. Then, oddly, the next day, they returned to her cedars, to her feeder. The following day—their *sweet sweet sweet sweet*s came again from across the road. Alternating days. El felt a partial victory. It was enough, she told herself. It was enough to see their splash every other day. To hear, up close, their songs. Four males, four females, feeding, singing, courting. It was enough to get through winter. It was enough.

•   •   •

Snow. Warm, wet snow. El cracked her window for the change in air. Trucks and pick-ups and cars of all kinds rolled slowly through the slush. It was warming. The snow on the roof nearly melted as it fell. The air, thick with moisture, brought every sound closer, like a whisper in her ear. She was now tuned to every sound, every shift in the breeze, every twist of a tree branch, every shuffle, every breath; she could hear them all, even under the muffling of the gray and brown and white and drear, but relentless, warmer flakes. She could hear the drop of the blue jay in the snow. She could hear the laughter from behind the trees across the road, the laughter from behind the windows behind the trees across the road. She could hear the tinkle of ice against glass. Marianne's sotto voce giggle. Jack Williston's murmuring. Lily's hands twitching and fluttering at her side as she practiced The Flight of the Cardinals and complimented Marianne on her green thumb. She could hear the light gray car two miles away, pressing foot to accelerator through the slush, ominous, cracking icicles off the eaves with its penetrating bass thumping. Underneath the bass thumping, the *sweet sweet sweet sweet* of a male as it came across to her cedar right on schedule. The female would be just a minute behind, now that they had become familiar with El's feeder, with the goldfinches, the chickadees, the blue jay. She could hear the *sweet sweet sweet sweet* from her cedar underneath the thump thump thumping gray and brown and white. The giggling, murmuring, twitching faded into the thick and swirling snow. She could hear a second *sweet sweet sweet sweet* as a second male arrived, calling his mate to the feeder. She could hear the thump thump thumping. She could hear the icicles cracking on the eaves. She could hear the *sweet sweet sweet sweet* as the male caught sight of its mate. She could hear the soft sweep of wings as the female swooped toward the cedar.

She heard the thump press.

She heard the sudden and deafening silence.

She couldn't hear her silent scream, the whoosh of her breath stolen. The whoosh as her skin drained to white and brown and gray.

Muttering Something about Raising Cain

I HEARD ABOUT CAIN from my great-grandfather. He knew everything: he could remember sitting on Parker's Ridge when the Redcoats marched up the valley with their machine guns blazing; he knew Johnny Appleseed when he had nothing but a bag of seeds and chewed on apple cores to get through the day. He said that, once, he'd shaken the hand of Ronald Reagan and "looked him in the eye." My great-grandfather even remembered the Greeks, back to when Homer escaped the Pilgrims and founded the town with his own name. The Pilgrims blinded Homer in the eyes so he couldn't see where he was going and had to wander a hundred miles. But Cain goes back further than Homer. Cain goes back to a time before even my great-grandfather was born.

It grew dark and he seemed to disappear in the creases the shadows created over his land. His land. The foothills of the Adirondacks, forty, maybe eighty acres. He sat in an Adirondack chair and surveyed the setting sun. It was his birthday, but nobody was saying how old he was. My Aunt Chee was ninety-nine and had been since I was four, but I think my great-grandfather was older than that. It was also the wedding day of one of my mother's cousins, and I think the last time there were so many of us together at one time. So many of us it would have taken a ge-

24

nius to know them all. My mother drilled us in the car, not that it helped much. There was my great-grandfather and great-grandmother. Their five children—four boys and my grandmother. My mother's aunts and cousins. Hundreds of cousins. I was only a couple of years younger than one or two of my mother's cousins, but they thought they were too old to be hanging around with me. My grandmother was the middle of the five. She married at sixteen and had my mother a year later. My grandmother's brothers didn't have kids until after the war, so I became the oldest of all my cousins like my mother was the oldest of all hers. I was too old to play with the babies and too young for my second cousins, who went off to neck with their dates once the sun began to set.

There wasn't much to do. The babies slept. Their parents cleaned up the paper plates from the picnic and pushed whole pies on one another to take home. Grandparents danced to the music from the radio in the kitchen and congratulated one another for surviving the war, their father, and another wedding. My sister had to pee but wouldn't—the outhouse scared her. My father watched from the picnic table, dazed by a dizzying shell game as one aunt after another rearranged the pies. My mother drifted between her brothers, my two uncles who hated each other and always had—because they had grown up in the same bed, in the same shoes, the same pants, the same urge to run away from home. They weren't twins. They just hated each other. My mother played along as she always had—with slaps to the tops of their heads. She was a lot older than her brothers.

In his Adirondack chair, on the little bit of a rise that was his backyard, in the center of his forty or eighty or one hundred acres, in the foothills of the Adirondacks, my great-grandfather struggled with his teeth. He sputtered a bit. He stomped his cane like a horse stomping flies. He shook his head. He stomped again. He sputtered. I was close enough to hear—"stupid people."

I was also afraid of him. He was cranky and crusted and shriveling before our eyes. Between stomps, he swung his cane about and didn't care where it landed. To top it off, that night he was fading in and out in the shadows. Someone lit an oil lamp and his skull flashed. I was stupid enough to encourage him.

"What?"

Of course I wasn't sure if he heard me, or that he wanted to, or that if he had he even knew who I was or cared. When we came back from the reception, we had all been paraded before him to be introduced, to pay our respects. He hadn't made it to the wedding; "It was too much for him," someone whispered, like a wedding was some kind of disease. He'd just waited it out in his Adirondack chair while his granddaughter was given away by his son. But he'd seen granddaughters given away. Four sons and a daughter produced so many granddaughters he could have gone into business. I'd heard that he'd gotten drunk for my mother's wedding and shook his cane at her, saying, "I don't want no goddam great-grandchildren now." That was the story, anyway.

So there I was, a goddam great-grandchild, standing before him with a mouthful of "whats?"

"What?" He said.

Or should I say "Wha?" He never had enough control of those teeth to get to the ts and ds.

"What?" I said.

"Wha?" He repeated.

We faced each other—me a skinny little kid, him a skinny old man—making wahs in the dark, me wondering about stupid people, him just confused and working his teeth until the oil lamp flared and he got a good look at me.

"Oh, Marguerite's—the wise ass."

Marguerite being my grandmother. I was about to tell him so, but I thought better of it. I'd already goofed once that night—probably the reason my great-grandfather remembered me at all and as a wise ass at that—by calling my grandmother's sister-in-law a "fat broad." My great-grandfather was the only one who'd laughed, and mostly because I'd caught it good from my mother. I'd tried to explain it was true, Hazel was a fat broad, and if my mother didn't believe me she could ask one of her uncles, because he'd said so and Hazel'd laughed. I got three or four pops on top of my head before she wheeled on her brothers.

I finally said "Stupid people?" and it got through. He waved his cane. He was pointing to the valley, the town in the valley, and by extension the world beyond, but I knew he meant the people on the hill too, the pie shufflers and dancers who generally had a good time every time one of theirs got married.

"Stupid people," he said. "Did you ever hear how there got to be stupid people? There weren't any stupid people at the beginning. Just smart people. Until one of them got too smart for his britches and got every last one of them stupid."

I didn't follow, but he said I didn't have to—I was stupid people too, but it wasn't my fault so I shouldn't worry about it. Which was good, because I was still worrying over why I'd gotten three or four good slaps over the head for joking around with my great-aunt. I think she was also my fifth cousin, twice removed. The rehearsals my mother ran us through in the car on the way to every wedding never stuck—aunts or great-aunts, cousins, second cousins, none of it made very much sense. In fact, it all sounded downright stupid and I was about to find out why.

"Nope, they didn't used to be stupid people. Smart people then. Damn smart."

He shook his head and did something like sucking air in between his teeth. The mosquitoes were out and I was slapping myself silly with them, but they didn't bother my great-grandfather one bit. They just lined up across his forehead like they were resting, storing up energy to come get the rest of us. Or maybe they were just up there digesting.

"Time was," he said, "when people had a memory. Now," he

stomped, "they can't remember a damn thing. It's worse all the time. You see George there," jabbing with his cane, "now he's the dumbest of the lot."

Actually, he was pointing at Warren. At least I think he was pointing at Warren.

"Couldn't remember a thing. Had to write every last thing down, that one did. Send him off to collect the eggs and he'd come back with grease on his hands. Changed the oil in the Ford. When I asked him where the eggs were, he wouldn't know. Wise ass like you. 'What would eggs be doing in the Ford,' he'd ask. No wondering about that. Knew what times the train came through every day though, and that's something. Though why anyone'd care about the 3:22 over the 3:44—all the same damn train, wasn't it?"

I heard my mother looking for me, but I sat quiet as I could, letting a mosquito bite straight through my arm because she'd know my slap clear across town. At least that's what I heard her say in the grocery once.

"You got a watch?" he said suddenly. The cane swung towards me. His watch hung from his wrist, the band big enough to slide over his hand.

I shook my head.

"Me neither." I was going to say something, but I thought better of it. It would have been the kind of thing my mother would have smacked me over the head about.

"Me neither." Working his teeth. I tried working mine, but all it did was make my nose itch.

"Charles there," jabbing his cane again, this time at Charles, I thought, but he was pointing at the whole valley too, so he couldn't really miss. "Charles there, he kept giving me watches. He'd say I needed to keep time. Like I needed to keep chickens. Can't eat minutes. Though they can eat you plenty."

He was working his teeth so hard I thought he was trying to eat the whole evening. It had his forehead moving he was working them so much, and all the mosquitoes were bobbing up and down with those teeth.

"I kept putting them in the drawer and he kept giving them to me. Had a whole drawer full. Finally just wore one—took a hammer to it and wore it. George asked me what time it was when the train was coming through. He thought it was late. How the hell did I know with a broken watch? Might as well not even had one."

A minute passed, maybe more. The pies must have been all away by then. My mother called again.

"Your mother married stupid," he said. "Stupid as they get."

This was a new one on me. My father taught at a university. The New York Yankees wanted him, but he went to college instead.

He leaned in close. His ears were humongous. His skin was kind of sliding off his face in the dark.

"Stupid as they get. Except maybe George there, and he didn't even go to college." I didn't know what to think except that my mother was calling, but he held me back with the hook of his cane and whispered through his teeth.

"But I didn't tell you how they all got stupid yet, did I?"

I waited. He shuffled around his pockets, moving his hand from one to the next. He looked like he was scratching himself all over, like the mosquitoes finally got to him. But he pulled out a piece of paper and showed it to me.

"There's the reason."

The paper was blank—or at least that's all I could see on it in the dark—nothing.

"This damn paper. That's the reason. People writing things down all the time so as they won't forget. Course they do. Why?" He stomped his cane good on that one. "Because they wrote it all down. Don't have memories worth ten cent. I'm not saying it's their fault. No, that goes back to Cain."

I didn't know what Cain had to do with it, but from the way he hooked me with that cane and pulled me close, I knew I was going to get the straight scoop.

"Adam named everything," his voice lowered, almost too low against the crickets and the pans and everything. "Before Cain came along, everyone just remembered everything. But then Cain comes along and he gets his britches all together. 'Adam,' he says, and he says it like that because he doesn't have any respect—no Cain never did. He'd march up to his father and say whatever he'd want. 'Adam,' he says, 'we can't remember all those names you said,' and you notice he says it like Abel was in on it, 'why don't we just write them down. That way we won't have to remember them—we can just look them up when we need them.'

"Well, Adam wasn't stupid. He ate the apple, remember, and he knew. Since he knew everything from eating that apple, he didn't need to be writing anything down because he already knew. He was used to being a fool, what with all that experience he had with Eve and the serpent. He knew he was a fool and he knew it didn't matter what he'd say, Cain would just use the paper anyhow and people'd get stupider and stupider. . . ."

There were a lot of fireflies out that night. Then there was Hazel and George leaning over me and someone shining a flashlight in my eyes and my great-grandfather in the dark muttering something about raising Cain. Then there was my mother asking where I got the pock mark on my forehead. I heard Hazel say it looked like words, only backwards. "The sign of the Devil," squeaked one cousin or another. George leaned in closer and I heard him read "U.S. Cane Co.," and Lois said "Imagine that." The next day a purplish bruise spread over the words so you couldn't read them anymore, and driving home my father and my sister and me made my mother crazy with trying to figure Hazel from Lois from Catherine from Lester from Warren from George. . . .

The Telephone Girl

ED JAMES WAS BOTHERED. "Bothered *greatly*," he'd tell you if you asked. But you wouldn't because you could tell right off if you bothered to notice. *Greatly* was his latest coup. He had, near as he could tell, coined a phrase, ingenuously invented a locution, and it turned more than a few heads. Some, like his cronies up to the college in Rome, favored it *greatly*. Others, like his mother, found it grating. He had hoped it would turn the head of Mimi Goncourt, for he favored *her* greatly. He still hoped it would, in fact. But for the moment, he was distracted. Bothered. Bothered *greatly*.

For the moment? He had been bothered for more than a week. His mother thought him moping, but it wasn't that at all. His mother thought a whole lot of things that weren't *at all*, he'd found out. Found out since he went up to the college. The Austro-Hungarian Empire did NOT, as his mother insisted, stretch from the Adriatic to the Baltic, hence Samuel Ward's "from sea to shining sea." The Amish were NOT a lost tribe of Israel banished from Europe by the Hapsburgs. Nor were the wigs worn by Washington, Adams, and Jefferson imported from Germany and woven from the hair of the great and powerful Maria Theresa, Queen of Hungary, Empress of Austria, and mother of the famed Marie Antoinette. Why would someone steal a dead woman's hair to make wigs for American revolutionaries? Precisely, says his mother.

31

Ed wondered about these things as he spied Mimi Goncourt in the window of the Homer Telephone & Telegraph Company. Her hair coiled and fell in thick cascades of gossamer. Each lock would provide ample material for a goddess's hairpiece. The Homer Telephone & Telegraph Company had hired Mimi as their telephone girl three months earlier. She replaced Velda Keusch in the window seat, Velda who quickly (some said *too* quickly) married Viktor Kusch. While Velda and Viktor cuddled and cooed, cozy in each other's arms in the apartment over the bank, Mimi graced the window at HT&T with a full view of Main Street. Main Street returned the blessing with a full view of Mimi. From just such consecrated ground was Ed able to watch her smile as she made her connections, her disconnections. Greatly so. From the west side of Main Street, the ampersand hid her smile. Ed walked to the east until one T overhung her like an umbrella. Connections. Disconnections. Secure behind the glass and safely seated under the umbrella that was the T, oh, it bothered him *so*.

Nothing his *mother* said on such subjects bothered him much, if at all. He had, however, read something that filled a crack in his mind. He'd read it up to the college. He hadn't thought much about it at the time, but now, as anyone with any brains at all could plainly see, it was a deeply troubling reading. He'd memorized it. Not on purpose. But it filled a crack in his mind, and filled it whole. With Mimi under the T in the window on Main Street, he found it swelling up, pressuring against the rest of his brain, incrementally increasing his pain until he was forced to actually mutter Edward Sapir's blasphemy:

The telephone girl who lends her capacities, during the greater part of the living day, to the manipulation of a technical routine that has an eventually high efficiency value but that answers to no spiritual needs of her own is an appalling sacrifice to civilization. As a solution to the problem of culture she is a failure.

As often as the passage was to occupy him in the coming days, it was the last time he produced it in its entirety; he lost sense as he gained clarity—for in the transmission from his tongue to his ear, the message was garbled. All he heard himself say was:

The telephone girl . . . is an appalling sacrifice to civilization.
. . . She is a failure.

Whether the ellipses represent mental static or simple inattention is immaterial. The message he *heard* could not fail to *bother* him. *Greatly* so. If, he thought, to himself of course, if he ever crossed paths with one saphead Sapir, well, he'd say something, some-thing . . . something . . . sapid. Something *sapid*. He let the words glide about his tongue for a good long taste and thought about serving it to his cronies up to the college. So distracted, he mo-mentarily forgot Mimi Goncourt altogether and would have forgot-ten what he was altogether about had not Clem Dinning hawked his name. This transported him to the present and rescued his foot from what would have been a certain soaking as it hovered above a deep and muddied puddle. The surveyor hawked again, and his momentary forgetting faded into eternity. Ed's attention returned to the present, the street and the pole in his hand. The surveyor waved him to the left and he shuffled a step. His foot re-ceived its due. Cheated once by the timely intrusion upon his reverie, Fate reasserted its claim in the form of a soaking. A slight smile slid across the surveyor's lips.

The paving of Main Street was a long time coming. The dust from the increasing number of automobiles speeding through the town on any given summer day had become a public hazard, said

Hirem ("the Mayor" appended some, "the Witless" added others, "Hirem Fire'm" intoned a few without cause—Mayor Hirem "the Witless" never hired, let alone fired, anyone ever). Hirem had addressed the city council: Hoving of Hoving's Hardware, Kesling of Kesling's Dry Goods, Musil of apothecarian fame, and Wilson of Frederick's Grain and Feed. Rischel from the *Ode* had been there as well, but it was hard to tell whether as a reporter or as a representative of the paper's owner. Rischel himself probably wasn't sure.

It had been the winter meeting of Homer's finest business minds. Hirem "the Witless" invoked the wrong problem at the right time—their memories of dust were ancient. The destruction wreaked by winter on Main Street was itself formidable and inescapable: cracks and holes emerged through the slush, and the mud that coated the floors of every merchant in town was deep enough to seed. But Hirem did have a point—if they paved, they wouldn't have to oil the street as they did every June and that would be "a savings amortized. . . ." With that utterance, Hirem drifted into pure babble. Economics was never foremost in his brain.

The merchants had enough smarts to see the merit in the plan and more than enough smarts to spread the cost to the general citizenry of Homer. Allan Dumfries ("the schoolteacher" said some, "the communist" groused a few, "simply addled" added others) tipped his cap to their skullduggeries when, several years later, the town began paving the rest of the streets. Then the merchants refused to pay, arguing that those who lived on the streets should bear the cost of paving. So began the Battle of Homer. Main Street fought First Street. First Street fought Second. Washington, Adams, and Jefferson Streets fought the numbers, the streets fought the roads, and the Rural Routes fought them all until Hirem Fire'em loosed a bottle of champagne amidst the flying fists and announced his engagement to Ellie Stiles with a toast about "a craving amorized." For one surprising moment, you could have heard a cork drop. Then someone mumbled something about a craving already satisfied and someone muttered something about raising Cain. After that, the battle evaporated with Hirem's bubbles.

Precisely where Ed James lived is neither here nor there, but he was hired by the surveyor as an apprentice for the initial project, with the promise of work later in the summer in charting the creek for a proposed dredging that would increase the flow of the proposed sewer once it was installed and connected. More to the point is that Ed stood on Main Street, shaking the water from his foot while attempting to steady the staff for the surveyor. He had been promised a look through the theodolite and an explanation of azimuths in general and of azimuthal equidistant projections in particular. It was an awfully technical business and he was more than happy to be learning something he couldn't learn up to the college. Greek and Latin were all right, he supposed, but this was something *greatly so*. He tried to comprehend what the surveyor had told him—that the pyramids and the Parthenon were surveyed with rocks and strings and water. He was baffled. As the water seeped from his shoe, he considered the fun he would have with azimuths and the slap he'd get from his mother if he told her what he was up to this fine morning. Better to be surveying azimuthals than projecting them, he mumbled, testing the sentence for its future impact on his cronies up to the college. The surveyor had his eye pressed to the theodolite and was waving at him. Ed waved back, and smiled—it was like getting his picture taken. The surveyor waved more emphatically, snapping Ed to attention. He shuffled to the right, his wet foot hardly registering the fresh soaking.

· · ·

Since his return from the college, meals at the Jameses' had been positively garrulous. Ed spent more words in a single question than his family did in an entire dinner. The evening of the day of his soaking, Ed asked his mother who the new telephone girl was. He knew her name, Mimi Goncourt, and he knew where the Goncourts lived, up the river just three miles, or thereabouts. He knew that they didn't used to live there—he had last walked the river with his friends several years ago and the old farm houses had been empty. They'd walked through the outbuildings and climbed in the loft of one of the barns, but they had been afraid to enter the houses. The Goncourts hadn't been there, nor had the Louÿs or the Maugérards, though he thought there may have been Goncourts once upon a time. He knew, for a fact, that the three families had moved to the United States from France only two (or was it three?) years ago and that none of their children had ever set foot in the school. In short, he said, he knew nothing at all.

The school teacher, Allan Dumfries, had been out to their farms. He told his students as much when the three families moved in, as part of an impassioned speech about America as haven for immigrants of all varieties of persecution, a speech that included pointed references to the French gift standing in New York harbor and the famed Lazarusian lines, "Give me your tired, your poor, your huddled masses yearning to breathe free." The new families were tired and poor and huddled, but they were free, said Dumfries. They simply wanted to be left alone.

"Who is Mimi Goncourt?" Ed asked again, watching his mother over a plateful of string beans and potatoes. He peered from under his eyebrows, or so he thought. In addition to coining phrases, he had been cultivating a "look." He wasn't sure what his look looked like except when his cronies clued him in. His mother, occasionally, let him know with a crack on his head that he was behaving like an idiot, but that didn't help him with his "looks." He did know, however, that working his eyebrows the way he did gave him headaches. He was thankful that he had grown used to them.

"They're from Alsace," said his mother. That was that. Straight answers meant "subject closed." Moreover, they usually contained a number of allegedly self-evident implications. Axioms, as his calculus teacher up to the college would have said. Ed knew now that he would have to discover the axiom(s) for himself. His mother's lips were white from pursing, his father hadn't a notion, let alone a clue, and Ed remained in the dark.

Without a plan, much less a clue, Ed set out for work the next morning fired by an impulse, an urge, a desire to learn more about the girl from Alsace. He watched her throughout the day as he tramped up and down Main Street. His cronies would have called it strutting, but they weren't about to revel in his new locutions so they had no call to be calling him out on his strutting. So he tramped. Had he had a pair of galoshes, he would have felt the image complete (not that he had a clear sense of the image he presented, or wanted to present). Tramping, however, was part of it, and he tramped Main Street like a professional tramp. As he did, he learned about azimuths and mensuration and meridians and verniers and angles of depression and elation and the tilt of Mimi Goncourt's head as she connected. Disconnected. As he tramped, he developed a plan. As he tramped, he developed a second. Two plans! *Greatly so,* he prided himself. How many people never even had ONE plan, let alone TWO? His feet remained dry. The puddles had evaporated.

At lunch, he enacted plan number one. Most people wouldn't have considered it much of a plan at all, but Ed was greatly impressed with himself. The surveyor straightened up from his hunched position behind the theodolite, stretched and announced the lunch break. Ed leaned the staff against the outside wall of the *Ode* and strode (his plan having taken shape, his tramps had become strideful) to the apothecary, which, as fortune had it, was nearly across the street from the offices of HT&T, the window of which displayed his lovely telephone girl. Fortune? Fortune be damned, it was all part of his plan.

Once inside, he lay a nickel on the counter and shuffled to the public telephone at the front of the store. He eyed it carefully, glanced across the street to be sure that Mimi was momentarily unoccupied, checked over his shoulder to be sure that he would not be overheard by the nearest customer, and, satisfied that all was proceeding according to his plan, picked up the receiver. His finger danced. His eyes were riveted on the girl who was separated from him by two thick panes of glass, the gulf that was the street, and the dust that was the world. He registered her every nuance, from the attitude she bore before the ring and her dawning, near instant, recognition of the electronic impulse, to the light on the switchboard before her. He noted the speed with which she pulled one jack from the bank of jacks, the artistry with which her hand paused, poised, the grace with which it was sprung by the fluid and dynamic movement of her rising arm. She was an angel bound to earth by the bundle of twisted fibers, filaments snaking into the firmament to ensnare his telephone girl. She fitted the jack to its appointed hole with such precision! He had not noticed this in his tramping up and down the street. He remarked the tilt of her head as she conducted this ritual, slightly to her left, his right, a lilting tilt as she weighed the profundity of her actions, inserted the jack, brought her eyelids together once as she drew in a short breath of air, all prelude to the parting of her lips and . . . .

"Allo?"

Allo? Suddenly, she was beside him, a jarring disjunction. Allo? The sound struck his ear all right, but his brain found it foreign, strange, unfathomable. Allo? The sound tumbled in his head, seeking a comfortable home, denied—vagrancy. He hung up. His plan thwarted before it began. Allo? What was that? A new locution? Greatly *so*. He hovered between utter incomprehension and unutterable affection.

In that hovering, he began anew, without a plan, without a clue, but with all the assurance of someone who has enacted a routine a thousand times or more, that is to say, without a thought in his head. He eyed the telephone, glanced across the street to be sure that Mimi was unoccupied, checked the positioning of the nearest customers, and removed the receiver. He marked every detail of the telephone girl, his telephone girl, from the attitude she bore before the ring and her dawning, near instant recognition of the electronic impulse, to the light on the switchboard that illuminated ever so faintly her internal glow. He remarked the speed with which she pulled one jack from the bank of jacks, her angelic elegance, her poise, the fluid and dynamic movement of her arm as it rose and fell, a fibrillic shimmer. She wove her coils with such precision. How had he not noticed this in his tramping up and down the street! He remarked the tilt of her head as she conducted this ritual, slightly to her left, his right, a lilting tilt as she weighed the profundity of her actions, inserted the jack, brought her eyelids together once as she drew in a short breath of air, all prelude to the parting of her lips and . . . .

"Allo?"

Again her voice struck him with the immediacy of her presence. Again comprehension eluded him. Again he was smitten with affection. Again he let the receiver drop with all the assurance of someone who has dropped a receiver a thousand times. He did not notice the irritated, nay *bothered,* yank with which Mimi Goncourt disconnected the jack. Nor did he notice the furrowed brow that she directed his way. He did note that he no longer had a plan, let alone two. Without them, he was adrift. Greatly so.

•   •   •

"This," said Clem Dinning, "this is the truly great achievement of modern man."

Ed was humped over the surveyor's scope, his eye pressed to the eyepiece, his back shooting pains in starburst patterns throughout his body, patterns that almost replicated the complicated set of crosshairs in the diaphragm of the theodolite. His eyebrows inflected against the glass. A headache crept from his eyes to the top of his head. Though nearly a quarter of a mile away, though nearly two hundred yards beyond the flag they planted to mark the edge of town, the stump in the crosshairs seemed close enough to touch. The hash marks on the lens were supposed to situate the stump precisely, but they floated in front of his pupils and signified nothing. He had a vague feeling that the entire scope, its tripod and lens, could be raised to accommodate his height without altering the stump's position in the world. It was a vague feeling, of uncertain origin, perhaps from his lower back. He also had the feeling, not from his back, that to suggest such a thing would be tantamount to blasphemy.

Suddenly, without warning, the stump exploded—twenty years of natural decay compressed into one moment and projected into space. It was there; it was flying apart. A full two seconds passed before he heard the concussion. Another two seconds passed before he heard the laughter.

"It's a sight, isn't it?" said the surveyor. He held a stick of dynamite in his hand, flipping it occasionally as he made his points.

"They think the skyscraper is the modern pyramid. The modern wonder of the world. It isn't. Not by a long shot."

Ed waited for the paean to nitroglycerin and was surprised.

"Roads. They're the modern wonder of the world. Paved roads. You mark my words, paved roads will do more for civilization than skyscrapers, ocean liners, and railroads combined. Their only competition is the telephone." He gestured vaguely at the HT&T building where Ed's graceful telephone girl made her connections, disconnections, "but," he said, "*that* can't do half what a paved road can do."

Now Ed was barely listening as the surveyor worked through a complicated algebraic proof that paved roads actually made distance, by which he meant the world, smaller by playing with time.

That, he argued, is the foundation of the modern wonders of the world. Do you think Einstein would have arrived at his theory of relativity as quickly as he did without paved roads?

The sound of Dinning's voice drifted on the air to mingle with the spasms emanating from Ed's back. He steadied his eye to the glass. The mention of HT&T had brought the scope around, as if by magic, as if the building were a lodestone drawing the point of a compass, compelling the needle to the building, to the telephone girl, his telephone girl. . . . Ed was not an idiot. He knew the telescope collapsed the distance between the viewer and the viewed, witness the explosion of the stump. But the sudden proximity of Mimi Goncourt, illusory as it was, was as concussive as dynamite. The board before her sparkled and glowed as the whole town of Homer conversed. The signals radiated and set Mimi's face ablaze. It was difficult, impossible, to discern whether the fire from her visage cast a veil, cast her own light upon the plate glass that separated her from the world of Homer, cast a glare that seemed to shear space itself into two disjointed realities, or whether that effect was due to the sun lowering in the west, its rays striking, reflecting, refracting against the glass. Perhaps two celestials met in Olympic contest, each veiled and veiling as they vied. His telephone girl and Apollo struggling against the glass, awaiting revelation. Polestar and sun; the star was truly stunning. Ed was drawn through time, through space, his eye pressed to the glass, rebuffed by the invisible plane. Ed was sacrificed at the altar of the goddess. Ed was smitten. Ed was a mess.

·   ·   ·

Ed stood at a boundary stone—a cement cylinder sunk into the ground and stamped with the county numbers, he knew that. He knew it was a hundred yards or more from the river because he could see the river and because he had walked the imaginary line through the brush from the river to the stone. He knew that behind him lay the town and home. Ahead—the Louÿs, the Maugérards, the Goncourts.

He knew he could not cross the boundary.

He hadn't set out to visit the Goncourts. Not, at least, so as he'd admit it to anyone, himself included. But his feet had brought him north along the river, and had brought him to the border. They would go no further. Not that he could admit that to anyone, himself included. Had his brain been in control this morning, it might have argued, had argued from practice, one of Zeno's paradoxes to explain his feet's inability to get where he wasn't going: to get there from here, one must travel halfway there. To get halfway there one must travel half way to halfway there. And so on. And so on through a compression of infinity until one walks away in disgust or intimidation. Such wasn't the response of one of his cronies up to the college as he'd tried to explain why the water in the water pistol pointed at his face would never reach him, thereby making the pulling of the trigger an effort in futility. Ed wasn't sure that he'd argued the point well enough. He'd tried it again with water dripping from his nose. When he failed once more to persuade the gunman of his folly, he resolved to join the debate club.

Ed's feet sensed the woods stretching into infinity and balked. Would roads shorten either distance or time, as Dinning argued? No. The gulf was immeasurable.

"Contemplating the Rune Stone?" Ed's feet nearly breached the gulf between earth and moon with the sudden and unexpected company.

"Rune Stone?" Ed asked.

"The magical markings of the ancient Germanic tribes, their spells and charms cast in stone."

Dumfries. Ed's heart returned to his chest. His feet still hovered an inch or so above the ground, ready for flight.

"It's just a corner stone marking a quarter," said Ed.

"Ah, marking a quarter," and Dumfries was off. "A quarter what? A quarter section? But what is that? What does this stone really remark? Does it apply to the world we see? Or does it apply only to the abstract world of numbers? Or," and this with a twinkle, "does it remark upon the mark itself?"

Ed had suffered four years with this man. It was largely upon Dumfries' recommendation that the college accepted him at all, having doubts, as they said, about the depth of his thoughts (which translated to the depth of his pockets, Dumfries said later, with a wagging finger and the admonishment—"Learn languages, you'll appreciate the power of translation"). Having already given over his brain to his feet in acceding to Zeno, he let his feet answer his former teacher by walking with him along the imaginary border to the river. The roar of the spring melt was already history. The river languished.

"The runes," continued Dumfries. "I recommend them. They're not so very unlike the marks you're learning now, though some would have otherwise."

Marks? Now? Ed was adrift.

"You're working for Clem Dinning, aren't you? Pay close attention to him."

Ed stood, silent, dumb. He wasn't sure he was ready for Dumfries.

"You mean he hasn't had you mapping?"

"We've been measuring Main Street," said Ed. "Mapping Main Street."

"And what kind of marks have you been using?"

"Lines."

"Lines. By all means learn your lines. He hasn't yet shown you the surveyor's runes?"

Ed shook his head. Dumfries took a stick ("a handy tool with infinite applications," he said) and began making marks in the sand.

He drew two parallels and added a quick series of short horizontals. "What's that?"

"The crosshairs in the scope?"

Dumfries smiled. A sly smile as if it appreciated his wise-assed answer. Ed hadn't meant to be wise-assed and was glad his mother wasn't there to deliver her crack to the top of his head. He looked again at the drawing—it still looked like the crosshairs in the scope.

"Funny guy," said Dumfries. "How about railroad tracks?"

Revelation was sudden and complete.

"Of course."

Dumfries drew tufts of grass. They looked just like tufts of grass and Ed complemented him.

He drew buildings and fences and stone walls, and Ed guessed. It got easier and easier once you knew the trick.

Dumfries began putting little holes in the sand, tiny little pointy marks.

"What's that?" he asked.

Ed couldn't begin to guess. It looked like a lot of little holes.

"Sand," said Dumfries. Ed winced, expecting his mother's crack on his head. There was a lesson in those points. He knew that, but he sure didn't know what it was.

Dumfries stood and stretched and looked to the sun.

"High time I'm getting on," he said. "I've got to give lessons up at the Goncourts, would you like to come?"

Ed stood still, mortified at the prospect, frozen, his brain quiet. He appealed to his feet. His feet refused to cross the border that was anchored by the stone. They didn't much care whether the border marked the land or numbers or involved themselves in the grand discourse of the universe. They wouldn't cross the line.

Dumfries left, whistling through the trees. Their new leaves filled the woods and Dumfries disappeared into infinity. Ed regained some consciousness. He began skipping stones. Oh, how they sailed and arced between hops. Mathematics was hard enough, he thought as he guessed at the azimuthals and altitudes of the skimming stones. Philosophy was impossible. *Greatly* impossible. He cursed philosophy. He cursed his feet. He cursed his own inaction. The marks in the sand mocked him. He bent to them, erasing them with a swift sweep of his hand. A solitary heron flew at tree height along the river, noting, no doubt, the water level and using it to measure the likelihood of fish. Inspiration struck and he grabbed the stick—replacing all the fancy symbols with a cryptic rune of his own: Μμι.

·   ·   ·

By the time he returned from the river, his resolve was set. He would call his telephone girl at home. That much was determined. The plan itself remained unformed. The Jameses had no contract with HT&T and so no connection to the world; Ed had to decide what phone to use in the reenactment of his earlier attempts to speak with his telephone girl. He also needed to identify when he would place his call. He had a vague feeling that had he dialed at that very moment he would have to go through kissable and gossipy Velda Kusch, who took Mimi's seat on the weekends. Velda's extra income helped meet the gap between the income and outgo of Viktor's earnings from Frederick's Grain and Feed.

His mother scolded him for escaping so quickly on a Saturday morning and handed him a list of chores that needed to be done. She pointed item by item at the list as she told him what to do, as if he couldn't read.

"Raking leaves," she said. "That means you take the rake and scrape all the leaves from the rose bushes in front of the house. See? It says that right there." A cracking punctuation.

"Washing windows," she said. "That means you take a bucket of warm water and a rag and scrub down the windows on the north side of the house, just like it says right there." A cracking punctuation.

"Burn the brush pile," she said. "That means you take the matches from the drawer in the kitchen and put the pile to fire. Be sure that you pay attention to it. I don't want to see the lawn catching fire just like I wrote there," she said with a cracking punctuation.

"I don't know how you'll get it all done today, what with your wasting half of it out who knows where."

There was to be a cracking, but Ed was in the shed rooting around for the rake. It wasn't there.

As he washed the windows, Ed recalled that the Goncourts didn't have a phone either.

By the time he had set the brush pile to a roaring blaze, he knew that he would have to reprise his earlier calls. He would have to wait until Monday, when Mimi occupied the window of HT&T. Not until then might he pursue his connection by using the apothecary's telephone.

•   •   •

Monday noon did arrive, despite Ed's near capitulation to the Zeno-tic infinity that was Sunday. His entrance into the apothecary was smartly engineered. He eyed the telephone, glanced across the street to be sure that Mimi was unoccupied, checked the positioning of the nearest customers, and removed the receiver. He marked every detail of the telephone girl from the attitude she bore before the ring and her dawning, near instant recognition of the electronic impulse, to the light on the switchboard that illuminated ever so faintly her internal glow. He remarked the speed with which she selected the jack, his jack, the jack representing him, her angelic elegance, her poise, the fluid assurance with which she tugged on his heart string. He remarked the tilt of her head as she conducted this ritual, slightly to her left, his right, a lilting tilt as she plunged into his soul, inserted the jack, brought her eyelids together once as she drew in a short breath of air, all prelude to the parting of her lips and . . .

"Allo?"

Again her voice struck him. Again comprehension eluded him. Again he was smitten with affection. Again he completed his routine with the hallowed and mechanical release of the receiver. It dropped the length of its cord and dangled—the penultimate solution to the problem of culture. He did not notice the irritated, nay *bothered,* yank with which Mimi Goncourt disconnected the jack. Nor did he notice the narrowing of her brow, vexation knit with nettles.

.   .   .

Clem Dinning offered Ed the scope again, and another lesson. Another lesson. There were so many parts to the infernal machine and more adjustments than one could imagine. It made no sense *at all.* Tighten one screw and a tree jumps three feet to the right. *This,* thought Ed, was what Saphead Sapir should have seen as the sacrifice to civilization—the measuring of the town—a map could be drawn in a hundred ways, each a function of one tiny adjustment; the vertical circle had a tangent screw, a zero adjustment, a spring box, and a horizontal axis adjuster. Of course the precise correlation of nature and number assumed that all the plates were screwed on tight, that the centering clamp was adjusted, and that the upper plate tangent screw, the lower tangent screw, and the leveling screw were all twisted to some approximation, but of what? It was enough that Ed knew which screw was which and, a baffling thought this, that he knew their names despite Dumfries' squiggles in the sand. So much depended on a steady tripod—were all the legs extended to equal lengths? Were they sitting on level ground? Screw up any of these and you get a different measurement—Main Street might run through Hoving's

Hardware, or the sewer might run through city hall. His head ached. He had a sneaking suspicion that Dumfries was to blame.

Ed set the tripod over the stake he had driven into the street the day before. He shuffled the legs of the tripod until the plumb bob hung a bare inch above the stake. The plumb bob hung menacing and nocent on its thread—an amulet, a charm, a fetish both warding off and embodying evil. The ancient surveyors were shamans with their weighted strings, staffs, and water levels. Ed was a shaman. A technological shaman.

Clem Dinning walked backwards, unfolding the chain link by link as he moved one hundred feet from Ed. He tugged it to its full length and then held the staff. Ed eyed the eyepiece to look through the centuries to the pyramids, the Parthenon.

Not only were they insuring that the road and the sewer would not veer from their appointed paths, they were also straightening the world. Main Street, and, consequently, the rest of the streets in town, had little curves, veerings, bumps, imperfections. The mayor, the city council, the surveyor, and everyone else, were bent on straightening everything to perfection. The road to Rome could not be squared with their right angles, of course, as it cut through the streets at a variance of nearly thirty degrees. Nor, of course, could the river road be reconciled with their projections. That is, at least, not without a bit of dredging and fill. So, the issue was not that it couldn't be reconciled, but that it wouldn't, considering the cost. . . .

Ed looked through the crosshairs at the surveyor and his staff. Something was odd and jarred him out of the past. The crosshairs themselves weren't straight—what had been two vertical lines side by side, with three horizontals equally dividing the space, what had been a rigid and primitive drawing of an insect scored into the glass, was no more. The verticals were all right, he supposed. They lined up quite well with the surveyor. But the horizontals were not right at all. They positively sagged! Ed removed his eye from the eyepiece and blinked. The surveyor called out for him to be sure that the lines were lining up with the hash marks on the staff. He looked again through glass and adjusted the verticals to the staff, but again, or still, the horizontals sagged. Had he broken the scope? But how? What could he say to the surveyor, who was pointing to the hash marks on the staff, hash marks he was to align with the now drooping lines? It was as if the world had gone momentarily soft on him.

Dinning confirmed the problem.

"Main Street would be fit for roller coasters on this accounting," he said, eye to the scope, as if it were the most ordinary problem in the world. He began unscrewing one end of the barrel and removed the ring that held the hairs.

He scraped away at the ring with his fingernail.

"Go find me a forked stick and a spider."

Ed sat back on his heels. A stick and a spider?

The surveyor repeated his instructions and sent Ed off to Hoving's Hardware. After a brief and baffling consultation with Hoving in which they puzzled over the surveyor's request, Ed was shown to the basement. He crept down the stairs, a jar in hand, stalking the unseen spiders.

Hoving was right, he did keep a clean ship, sweeping not only the floors but also the walls once a week. Even so, Ed could see traces of webs between the joists. "Even *so*," he muttered, testing, tasting, and spitting it out, as he retrieved the step ladder and began his search in earnest. The first web was obviously abandoned. It fluttered lazily when he blew on it. Two or three feet further down, however, he saw something more promising. He descended the ladder, aligned it with the joists with all the technical mastery his precise work with the theodolite had required. He remounted the ladder.

He blew softly on the web and found it intact. The rippling gossamer also revealed the spider, though not as he had expected it to. He had thought, a thought barely articulated, that the gentle disturbance caused by his breath would simulate the disturbance a fly might make. The spider, so alerted to his dinner, would dash out to secure the fly. Such was his plan. Instead, he saw the spider retreat. In his wonder, he impaled himself on a nail. Even so, Ed quickly jarred the creature.

He emerged from the basement as if from a battle—glorious and triumphant. His hair was covered with cobwebs as if he had fought a dozen spiders, each larger than life. More serious was the puncture in his head from one of the numerous nails protruding at odd angles though the floorboards as if a carpenter had gone insane while installing the underflooring. The nail that caught him unaware had scraped a bit of his hair right out of his head and held it as a trophy. Even so, the spider sat in the jar, its legs, like the nails, at all angles but drawn to its body much as his telephone girl sat behind her glass, cords drawn and waving as she made her connections, disconnections. Greatly *so*? Ed was disconcerted. Dinning barely looked into the jar before sending Ed off for the forked stick.

"Watch carefully," said the surveyor when Ed returned. "This is something you'll want to know."

He poked the stick into the open jar and pushed it about a bit until the spider climbed on one of the forked ends. He withdrew the stick and held it still so the spider could get its bearings. Then, ever so gently, Dinning jiggled the stick. It was a perverted sort of water witching. The spider dropped toward the ground, hanging by its thread. Dinning squatted, the spider dangled, Ed sat openmouthed and silent. As Dinning began to slowly twist the stick, the spider slowly spun his thread. He twisted such that the thread was taunt and wound about the fork, two, three, four times around the tines. The spider continued to spin, hovering, stationary, a full foot from the ground until the surveyor broke the thread. The spider dropped.

"That ought to do it," he said, and rummaged through his case with his free hand. He removed a small jar of shellac. He fit one of the threads to the hash marks on the diaphragm and applied a small drop of shellac to secure it. He repeated the process for the other two sets of hash marks, an odd and abominated web weaving. The shellac dried, he returned the ring to the scope and satisfied himself that his work was neatly done with a long and steady look through the lens.

Ed searched for the spider, but it was gone.

•　　•　　•

Quitting time. They stowed the equipment in Dinning's truck. Dinning drove off, past the hardware store, past the hotel, dust rising and filling the street as he turned onto the road to Rome. The sun still hung above the buildings and cast its glare on Kesling's Dry Goods, the Homer *Ode,* and Homer Telephone & Telegraph. Ed could barely see the lettering with the glare, let alone what those windows displayed. He shuffled into the sun, west, homeward, and as he scuffed, he kicked a piece of quartz, rounded by the river, covered in the dirt of Main Street, and just about the size of the plumb bob. He shuffled, scuffed, and kicked at the quartz. Semiprecious silicon dioxide, Dumfries would have said. Liable to hexagonal fissures. Talismanic. Ed wasn't sure what *he* would have said as the quartz wrapped itself into his thoughts, its fissures entangled in webs and bits of string and water levels and water mains and the straightening of Main Street and the streets of Homer. Rock. String. Water. His thoughts stymied by connections. Disconnections.

He stood opposite Homer Telephone & Telegraph. His telephone girl sat behind her glass in the center of a tangle of wires. The wires were their own gross abomination of a web, though markedly different from the calculated parallels woven by the surveyor or the jagged hexagons buried in the quartz. The wired snarl surrounding his telephone girl was without order, as though the spider were drunk, or insane, or patterning its web on the flight of flies.

Then the unconscious enactment of a vague idea, born not of his brain, not of his back, not of his feet, but of his hand. His hand recognized the mineral in ways unimaginable to his brain or back or feet, and he bent to pick it from the ground, to cradle it in his palm, fingers curled, coiled. A dawning. Not a eureka, but the slow creeping recognition of a neural pattern, like the gradual rise of the sun, presaged by the shift of color, from murky blue black, to hazy blue green, to the rosy glow in the eastern sky. Rose quartz. His hand hefted its weight. His fingers squeezed before they released it to the sky.

It soared. *Greatly* so. Without his having projected an azimuthal. It soared. *Slowly* so. Without a hitch or a hesitation, it bridged each half distance, connected one moment with the next, spanned the infinite. It soared. *Lazily* so. Without a care, it drifted toward the only wonder of the world. It peaked. Water. Rock. String. Sun and stars righted in the alignment of the cosmos. It fell. A stupendous crash.

Time begins anew.

In the first moment, a hundred fractures race through the plate glass, a hundred threads connecting, the alphabetic HT&T obliterated by the ever-conjoining, all-communicating fissures, a godlike spider weaving the world in an instant.

In the second moment, a thousand threads disconnecting, an explosive starburst of glass, the fabric of the world rent.

She twists in her chair. Startled. Stunned. Her mouth a frozen "Allo." Her brows knit. Her ears, her eyes, her mind register the incomprehension so familiar to Ed. He raises his hand, upright and open and empty, his palm to her in a tentative wave, his palm to her to connect his own unutterable incomprehension, his affection, to connect in the simple gesture of the hand. The telephone girl, his telephone girl, raises her own hand in an expression already tied to the beginnings of a smile.

• • •

Lucy's Eggs

1

LUCILLE CHARLOTTE BARTON DELANO had fourteen Araucanas. They were gold and rust and bold and tall and so very different from the Hamburgs and the Dorkings that dominated the
Homer homesteads. After church one Sunday, nearly a week after
her original Araucanas, her first hens, arrived in all their splen-
dor, Lucy's best friend, Ethel, sat on the small and tended square
of grass outside the rectory, spread her dress such that it formed
a near perfect circle about her (for all the world looking as though
she was a swan floating upon stilled waters), and told Lucy that
Araucanas came from South America, probably from Chile.
Ethel's attitude was compelling, as were the curve of her neck, the
tilt of her head, and the lilt in her voice. Lucy hoisted her skirts
and squatted to join Ethel, who was lost in her reveries, but in her
heart she knew her Araucanas really came from Rome, and were
the reward for her diligence and determination.

So *much* diligence. So *much* determination. A summer of
mucking Temperance's stall had proven to her father that she was
worthy of a small flock and capable of their care. It had been a
long summer. Temperance was a Belgian mare and a prodigious
producer of piles upon piles upon piles. Furthermore, she preferred to deposit her piles in her stall rather than the paddocks or

pasture so that Lucy was responsible for nearly all of her Antaean output. Lucy was small. She was small enough, in fact, that she could walk under the mare's belly without ducking. She was too small to maneuver the wheelbarrow, so, every morning, she filled a large basket and dragged it down the short slope to the edge of the family garden with two hands in a backward shuffle that forced her nose into the manure. It often took three or four trips to empty the stall of manure and the old straw that was saturated with the mare's urine. The urine filled her tiny nostrils and set her wobbling. Once her head cleared, she would rinse the basket in the creek, pause for just a moment to watch an undigested oat spin and swirl in the water, and set it upside down to dry on the stump outside the barn. This was the signal to her father that she had completed her part of the bargain. After several deep breaths of air, she would run off to help her mother.

Her reward for her Herculean labor was a small flock of Araucanas. One morning, her father set out for Rome behind Temperance and Chastity, who pulled the wagonload of the farm's recent production: late-season vegetables, three barrels full with potatoes, a few bundles of firewood, and four creels of fine ash strips woven by her mother and coveted by the sportsmen who summered in the region. Her father could have delivered these goods to Kesling and the other merchants of Homer, but early antagonisms involving a cash-recording machine forever soured him on the town. He was certain that the mechanism was fixed: every time Kesling pressed an amount ending in five, the machine added a dime—five cents became fifteen cents, fifteen became twenty-five, twenty-five became thirty-five, and so on, in what her father called the slickest moneymaking machine since the mint. Her father distrusted the mechanism. Kesling refused to figure an exchange on paper. And so evolved a lifelong enmity that made the fifty-two-mile journey worth every step.

He returned the next afternoon with the wagon just as full:

vegetables exchanged for two pairs of shoes, firewood brought flour, the four ash-stripped creels transmuted into a shovel, a bolt of calico, a lantern, and oil. Crowning them all with a burst of light was a small wooden cage containing six golden pullets! Lucy spotted them from her room as Temperance and Chastity quickened their pace. She left her room at a bound and burst from the house to greet them.

Six golden pullets!! They were to be *her* birds, hers to tend, hers to care for, hers to protect, and hers to keep separate from the free-ranging Hamburgs and from the geese who had divided themselves into two flocks—grays banded with grays, whites with whites—that patrolled the yards and honked and hissed and spread their wings upon encountering each other. The arrival of her pullets set the geese into an apoplectic frenzy, as if the devil's own had suddenly appeared in a fiery augury of the apocalypse. Six alloyed phantasms to herald the end of the end! The geese positively swooned.

Six golden pullets!! She could hardly contain her joy as her father set the small cage on the ground. She peered and clapped and danced and clucked. She threw herself to the ground and nearly crawled inside the cage until she was face to face with twelve fiery eyes that measured her over six bright yellow beaks. She cooed softly as she stroked their head feathers, feathers so fine and so much softer than the puffed tips of pussy willows or the bursting fronds of cattails. She immediately set about naming them: Victoria, with her emboldened eye; Catherine, an extra red streak running down the middle of her breast; Elizabeth, who kept her head low to the ground; Winifred, a single yellow feather atop her head; Gwendolyn, whose ruffled tail feathers could not be smoothed; and Maude, the softest and smallest of all.

With their naming, the birds themselves seemed to know that they were special. Lucy made a pen and changed their straw every day. The pullets strutted and plumed under the attention, submitting themselves to Lucy's cradlings. Their eyes, gold and bright and attentive, darted about the yard in a proud and possessive survey of all that was rightfully theirs.

Even as pullets, they were stronger than the seven-year-old girl. The merest stretchings of their wings, preliminary to their fledgling attempts to fly, were enough to bruise her arms. As they grew and became less docile in her hands, their incessant fussings and flappings became positively painful. The birds tolerated her cooings, her soft pettings, her cradlings; they tolerated Lucy herself. But with the rest of the world, they were not nearly so quiet, nor charitable. They swelled their breasts and thumped their wings whenever the family spaniel approached. They stretched their necks and stomped their feet whenever Lucy's father neared the pen. They ran with heads low, nearly spitting with their contempt, when the sun rose each morning. For all their territorial warring, the white and the gray geese kept their distance from the Araucanas' pen. The Hamburgs bumbled about the yard, oblivious to the geese, oblivious to the Auracanas. Once, with the utmost determination, with a combination of sheer will, a swirling updraft, and the utter conviction that she could fly, Gwendolyn leapt the fence that kept her from her rightful place in the world. Once freed from Lucy's fence, she fairly flew at the hapless Hamburgs, a blazing red and gold streak that sent the silvery black birds in all directions. Gwendolyn cut one from the flock and, whether from the belief that she had found a choice morsel of worm or whether from sheer spite, decimated the Hamburg's tidy rose-colored comb.

Retribution was swift. Lucy's father snatched the Auracana by its feet and abruptly snapped its neck. He then left it in the yard, a lesson for his daughter.

What she learned horrified her. At dinner, her father described the Araucana's transgression, its threat to the family and the production of the farm, and his meting out of justice. Lucy sat, still, silent, fighting every muscle that twitched and jumped, fighting the tears she felt welling up in her eyes. Her father continued to eat. His knife scraped against his plate. His fork rose and fell with some precision. Lucy twitched. Her father chewed and ruminated. His fork rose and fell. His knife scraped the plate. His fork scraped against his teeth.

Lucy barely breathed.

Eternity hovered, suspended between the rise and fall of the fork, between inhale and ex.

Finally, her father set his fork to the left of his plate and his knife to the right. Lucy, released, bolted from the room, her tears flying as freely as her feet.

She found the Hamburgs in a merry feast. Every muscle in her body, every twitch, every jump, every breath that had been stilled as her father maintained his order, came together into one enormous scream. The Hamburgs flew about, wings beating in all directions, wings beating themselves into an unutterable chaos.

It took nearly an hour, but she finally collected all of the feathers that had been scattered by the Hamburgs and the wind, and, with a trowel, dug a shallow grave for her dear Gwendolyn. She cried for two days, forgetting all else as she lavished her attention on the remaining five. Temperance quietly filled her stall, stomping her manure into a fine veneer, threatening with her massive feet the flies that hounded her. Winter accomplished what her feet couldn't. With the freeze, the flies died.

With the winter came new surprises. Victoria and Winifred were roosters. They tested themselves against each other over the frozen water bowl and chased Elizabeth, Catherine, and Maude about the small coop that Lucy and her father assembled in the barn. Her father cursed the merchants of Rome for their ignorance. He towered over her, over her birds, with his hands on his hips. A hen is a hen is a hen, he said with some disgust.

The second surprise was the first egg. It appeared suddenly, as if by magic, on the winter solstice. It was perfectly round and more exquisite than anything Lucy had imagined when she first began dreaming about Araucanas and their pale blue eggs. Indeed, as the season moved into February and the eggs came with more and more regularity, she noted their elongated, "egg-like" shapes, their bumps and their freckles. The solstice egg was an anomaly, something she came to recognize over the years. Solstice eggs were always different. Sometimes double or triple yolked, sometimes perfectly round, sometimes nearly tubular, their colors were often dramatically different from the eggs of the rest of the year—a rich green or a reddish blue. Atalanta would predict the great 1906 San Francisco earthquake with a solstice egg whose yolk was already broken as she laid it. L'il Dickens, born with the century, would presage the horrors of the Great War with her nearly blood-red solstice eggs. This first egg, however, was to be cherished.

Lucy discovered it when she fed in the morning. It was a glorious morning. The snows had not yet arrived. The grass crunched under her feet as she skipped from the house, across the yard to the coop. The sun paused in the sky. The world was perfectly still, as if holding its breath, anticipating Lucy's surprise. She lifted the latch, opened the door, and stepped inside to find, at her feet, *The Egg!* Her surprise was tempered by the shock of its abandonment—in the middle of the coop, in the middle of the floor, where it could be broken by anything! She leapt forward to snatch it from the cold floor. The birds watched her indifferently in a line from the roost. They jockeyed for position. They measured the distance between the bar and the floor as though they had never jumped it before, and then, one by one, descended with a cluck and a squawk amidst a flurry of beating wings. One by one, they fluffed themselves and rearranged their feathers. One by one, they cocked their heads such that each had one eye fixed on their mistress. One by one, they circled the girl, marching counterclockwise with a nearly demonic and clocklike precision. Lucy's eyes grew wide and she began to twist in place, following her birds, Victoria becoming Catherine becoming Elizabeth becoming Winifred becoming Maude. A dizzying becoming. One could argue that their behavior was entirely ordinary. They were hungry. It was feeding time. Each morning without fail, the young girl would enter the coop and strew corn. Each morning without fail, the birds would leave the roost for the floor and scratch about her feet as they awaited their grain. This morning, however, their circling and scratchings were positively malevolent. Lucy clutched the egg to her chest. The Araucanas circled and circled, their heads cocked, their golden eyes gazed into hers, measuring the distance, calculating, deciding whether her moist white orbs were truly the tasty grubs they appeared to be. Lucy grew dizzier and dizzier under their gaze. Maude ruffled her feathers. Catherine fluffed. Lucy screamed. Temperance snorted. Chastity raised a foot and set it down, her hoof scraping the stall on its way. Lucy bolted, the egg firmly in her hands.

She ran the yard. Hamburgs scattered on the wing. A gust of wind caught the tops of the maples and stirred them with a gush that urged her on. She flew into the house and up the stairs to her room, terrified the birds were after her. She slammed the door against their malevolence and looked frantically for a place to hide the egg from their searching eyes. She found a small wooden box and tucked herself away in her closet, with her egg in the box, her box in her hands, her hands in the closet, in her room, in the house, and reverberating through all of them, the horrid thumping of her heart.

By afternoon, her heart had quieted to match the steady breathing of sleep. By supper she was calm, calm enough to cup the egg in her tiny hands, to run her fingers over its smooth exterior, to warm it against her stomach. She took a small woolen sock and circled it in the box and laid the egg ever-so-gently in the center. As the house quieted for the night, she wrapped herself in her quilt in the middle of her bed and slept long and deep.

The third surprise came with Epiphany. It was a not-so-sudden, creeping revelation, forestalled by a series of distractions. There was the excitement of Christmas. Her father led her by the hand to the coop to show her the nest boxes he had crafted for the birds. She nearly squealed when she saw that he had carved their names into the front board on each one: Victoria, Winifred, Elizabeth, Catherine, and Maude. Then she saw that her birds were all mixed up—Victoria was in Elizabeth's box. Elizabeth was in Maude's. Catherine and Winifred had switched places. Maude was left alone, on the bar. Lucy rolled her eyes at her father, as though he should have known, and immediately set to fussing with the hay in the boxes and to matching each bird to its box. The hens tolerated her excitement. The roosters, less so.

Her mother had made her an egg basket. It was a perfect surprise even though Lucy herself had helped in the basket's making, for she had gone with her mother down the road three quarters of a mile in late summer to cut the willow strips. Her mother had hummed along the way, a waltz, while Lucy swooped, one two three, and stepped, one two three one, and stumbled, three one two, and laughed at the beauty of her mother's voice, all the more lovely for its lack of words, for its purity of sound, for how it resonated through the woods. The willows awaited as the pair approached with their odd dance, sweeping in contretemps to the movement of a grand, five-trunked box elder that swirled with the wind. Lucy's mother produced a small serrated knife, and the two took turns cutting through several branches that were thicker than Lucy's wrists. The first cuts were the easiest; the edges of the blade sank quickly into the outer bark that protested the violence with a series of small wrinkles and through the several ringed layers to the core. Once half-way, however, the wind swept the willows' branches and they squeezed the small knife and held it, and Lucy and her mother had to tug and push at the branches to stop their pinching. "Willow witches," said her mother. Lucy's heart skipped a beat, even as she refused to believe. In all, they cut five and dragged them home, their earlier waltz now a swooshing trudge as twenty feet of willows swept away their footprints.

Lucy had helped with more than the gathering. Once home, they trimmed the thinnest shoots from the branches and then cut them into two-foot sections. Once home, the cutting was easier, at least at first, for the willows again protested by filling the serrations with their woody fibers. Together, mother and daughter cut and soaked and peeled into strips the caning for two chairs. Her mother made sure to save enough for the egg basket, and wove it in the interstices of her day when Lucy was out of the kitchen, out of the house, and playing with her birds.

The basket was, of course, perfect. It was long and deep, like an oriole's nest, and slightly tapered on the inside at the bottom to prevent the eggs from rolling around. Her mother had lined it with dried moss to protect their shells. She had stained the willow by rubbing raspberries and cranberries deep into the wood. The basket glowed red against the firelight.

It was perfectly timed, for there was the sudden proliferation of pale blue eggs. The hens laid two, sometimes three, a day and Lucy found herself completely absorbed by the duties they required. Each morning, she lifted the egg basket from its hook on the porch and hurried across the yard, anxious to discover how many eggs her hens would give her. If she was careful not to make a sound as she crossed, as she slipped the latch to the coop's door, she might be lucky enough to see which hen was sitting in which box. This was her only clue to which hen laid which egg. The slightest sound, however, would have the birds in a line on the bar, waiting for her entrance and for the mash she made for them: warm bran and peas. They never ate all of the bran, and there was a growing frozen patch in the middle of the floor. She discovered that Victoria liked Maude's box and would sit on the egg there, even though Victoria was a rooster and shouldn't want to nest. Lucy would chase Victoria from the box, pick up Maude, stroke her tiny ear feathers, and set her on her egg. Maude preferred eating peas to warming her eggs, however, and would quickly leave the nest for the floor.

Lucy cupped each egg, fondling it gently, turning it slowly in her hands to note each freckle. She was at once anxious and excited on the days when all three hens laid an egg; two eggs would bump against each other in the basket—three would crash about. In the thin, cold winter air, she heard each coming together of shells and feared their cracking. To muffle their movement, she held the basket close to her body. Walking to the house took twice as long as her scuttle to the coop. A warm spell struck terror in her heart. The yard turned to mud, and she could barely step without her feet sliding in all directions. Once, she fell, soaking herself in the cold, wet muck, and almost burst into tears. But she only had one egg in her basket and the moss saved it.

When she was safely inside, she would set her eggs on the table and carefully bathe each one. She soon discovered that she could tell them apart. Maude's eggs were always smaller than Elizabeth's and Catherine's. Elizabeth's had more freckles. Catherine's were a slightly paler shade of blue. She washed them twice, sometimes three times, just to be sure that they were clean. She liked the way they filled her hands. She liked their warmth. As her hens continued to lay, she lost herself in the eggs. One dozen, two dozen, and more—she was mesmerized by the pale blue orbs, blind to the rest of the world, the horses, her chores, and even her parents. She was fully under their spell.

Revelation was not sudden. There was the creeping premonition, felt mostly as she climbed the stairs at night to slip into her bed, a creeping portent that hung over her bed as she tried to sleep, spooked by the shadows and the mice in the walls. It became heavier when she dressed in the morning, fumbling through her closet for her skirts and stockings and shoes. Over several days it grew weightier still and hung about her; she felt it, something was in the air. She thought she could actually smell it, so much that one evening, after coming in from the barn, after tickling Temperance's belly with a strand of hay such that the mare's nose twisted in delight, she wrinkled her own nose to test the air. The feeling grew as she readied herself for bed, until she hid herself under the quilt her grandmother made, the last quilt her grandmother had made before she died. It was a crazy quilt, made of every scrap left in her grandmother's possession, scraps sewn in forty ever-swirling circles, scraps from every year of her life, scraps from her wedding dress, scraps of wool, of velvet, of silk, of cotton, scraps arranged as if her grandmother were thumbing her nose at the steam-powered textile machines that spun out of control and stole half a hand from her husband—Sew this! she seemed to say. That night, the interlocking circles contributed to Lucy's uneasy sleep. A series of dreams brought her to the edge of something, a wall, an overhang, the roof of the barn, a door. Each time the dream broke off suddenly with a waking start that left her more unsettled than ever before.

With morning, she was nearly afraid to get out of bed, but more afraid to remain with the vestiges of her dreams. With a quick intake of the thickening air, she bounded from beneath the quilt to her closet, stopping suddenly in alarm, shaking herself, shaking off the dream, but she wasn't dreaming, and the evil that seeped from under the door was visible, palpable. She stretched her hand out, to touch the evil, and brushed her fingers against the knob. The door swung on its hinges, protesting with a creaking that set her hair crawling. As it swung open, a noxious odor flooded the room and nearly swept her away. She held her nose and took a step forward: buried in the back of her closet, behind her summer dresses, under three stuffed bears—her solstice egg. Forgotten with the excitement of Christmas and the sudden proliferation of eggs, her solstice egg had revealed itself with an odor so horrible, so thick, so pungent, so pervasive that she was forced to sleep the next four winter nights with her window opened wide. Epiphany.

•　　•　　•

Lucy's nose wrinkles with the faint imprint the smell has made upon her olfactory system. The wrinkling is unconscious, born from the too-numerous discoveries over the years that her hens have gone to the greatest lengths to hide or misplace their eggs. Certain hens, Weewaw and Jaunty Girl in particular, developed the habit of hiding their eggs from Lucy and from the periodic invasions of rodents. Eventually, their hiding places were revealed by the odor. The rats themselves contributed to the smell when they forgot to eat their stolen bounty in their mad rush to steal the world and tuck it away in their runs. There was little Lucy could do about the eggs left to rot in their runs but to endure and to wait.

Her left hand rises, just as unconsciously, brushes the tip of her nose, and descends, joining her right hand in a communal drying on a dishtowel. Lucy stands at her kitchen sink, washing eggs. Though difficult to notice, her lips are pursed under her unwrinkled nose. Josh Kesling, whose father sustained such enmity from her own, and several of his contemporaries have said that she has no lips at all; the younger Kesling, now fifty-four and filling out like the sacks of flour that line his walls, once commented that she has come to resemble the hens she dotes so much upon. That would be unkind. Her hair has nothing of their fire, nor had it ever. It has softened over the years, from mouse brown to mouse gray. Her eyes have softened as well with the passing seasons. Indeed, her entire visage reveals a quietude born of her years, with the sole exception of her lips, for Kesling and his contemporaries are in error: Lucy's lips have born the hardships—every stray dog, every wayward indignity, every season gone sour has gone straight to her mouth. Through it all, she has held her tongue. Her lips are pursed as she stands at her kitchen sink.

She is washing the eggs. One is ever-so-slightly bad and she can tell which, even at this early stage. She carefully sets it to one side, a fleeting thought of Josh Kesling, a fleeting unpursing of her lips into a smile? She is washing the morning's bounty, eight eggs from her fourteen chickens, collected in the same basket her mother gave her more than fifty years ago. The basket sits to her left on the counter. Several willow strips have broken and catch on the oddest things. It is dry, brittle-dry. Every year, she soaks it in water. Every year, it seems even drier. With the soakings, the raspberry and cranberry stain has faded—the basket is nearly the color of her hair. Next to the basket, a half-dozen eggs await the water. They lay on the counter like gems fresh from the mine. On the counter, to her right, one glistens in the morning light. In her hands, she can feel three slight ridges that hold the water for one extra moment. It is Josephine's; she knows from the feel of it alone. When she has finished washing her eggs, she will sit at her kitchen table and eat toast with jam and drink coffee. The eight eggs, of course, are six too many, even after taking away another one or two for baking. Every few days, she has a full dozen to send away. A full dozen to send away.

The house is warm. Nearly stuffy. She has opened windows to catch the southern breeze. It carries the warm, muggy air and fills the parlor with humidity. The kitchen, on the north, remains hot.

Melvin is haying the field across the road. The scent of the fresh-cut alfalfa drifts through the house. It is a wonderful smell, the smell of late June, the smell of barns in the fall, the smell of the fairgrounds. Lucy sets her apron aside and steps outside to the front porch for a richer inhale. She wonders, idly, whether the jugglers will be at the fair this year. The first year she exhibited, four jugglers, costumed and frenzied, descended like weasels upon a chicken house. They snatched the eggs from her basket and began tossing them through the air. It had taken her breath away and she stood, paralyzed, watching the soft blue eggs soar, round and round, disappearing altogether against the soft blue sky, only to reemerge as if by magic. As if by magic, she thinks, they made their torture appear marvelous—for it was torture to see her hens' eggs fly, without wings, knowing that at any moment they might land, that the jugglers might slip, that she might breathe and disturb the delicate balance.

She didn't breathe. The jugglers caught the eggs without incident. Everyone clapped and laughed and applauded her hens and her hens' eggs and she didn't know whether to laugh or cry. Years later, she discovered that such shakings ruin an egg just as surely as dropping it on the ground. They don't separate as well for baking after they've been shaken. Sometimes it breaks the yolk inside the shell. Years later, she cried.

The day after the jugglers trespassed, Peter Ganton, William Moore, and George Blackman raced through, snatching up whatever was handy and tossing it into the air, as if *they* were the clowns, as if *they* were the jugglers. It didn't matter what was on a table, they made their play. Peter reached for her eggs, but Lucy screamed. The scream was a mild diversion. Peter grabbed Winifred. Lucy screamed again. The other boys threw vegetables and rabbits about the tent. Winifred beat his wings against the boy and pecked at his head. Peter let go, let loose a cry of his own, fell, toppling the table and its display over on Lucy. It crushed one of her eggs and she sobbed for two hours while the adults tried to restore order to the tent.

That first fair presented her with a horrible problem. Exhibitors were only allowed to show two chickens—one rooster and one hen. The choice was difficult, but in the end she selected Winifred and Elizabeth, though she wouldn't allow herself to say why. She had no favorites, except for Maude. Winifred's extra-fine cheek feathers were not a reason. Nor was the coy head turn Elizabeth always gave when Lucy came near. No, she had no favorites and no reasons for selecting the two she did. She hugged Victoria and Catherine as she left for the fair. Victoria pecked at a mole on her cheek. Catherine fussed and pouted in her arms. Maude understood and sat quietly in Lucy's lap as the young girl stroked her comb.

There was a second problem, of course. She was allowed to bring as many eggs as she wanted, so she'd soaped and rinsed a full half-dozen for all of Homer to appreciate. The problem was how to display them. Her egg basket was too deep for anyone to see anything at all! She finally settled on an old plate, and gathered a handful of straw so that the plate might look like a nest. Then she had a spark of inspiration. She raced to the trees by the creek and gathered enough moss to cushion all six eggs. It took her three days to get everything just so, but her display was perfect. Maude's egg sat in the middle, slightly higher than the five that surrounded it. She arranged the other eggs like a star with five tips—Catherine's light blue eggs at the top and the bottom, Elizabeth's more freckled eggs to the sides, and all of them pointing in toward Maude's perfection. She carried the plate everywhere she went, in growing pride, showing it to her chickens for their approval, to the horses for their snuffled pleasure, and showing off to the Hamburgs and the geese. The geese were happy to see the wagon finally leave for the fair.

The fairgrounds were laid out in a giant oval. Lucy noticed right away that it was egg-shaped, or nearly so, and so knew that the fowl were the rightful kings and queens of the fair. The grandstand, large enough for fifty people, lined the south side of the oval, designed so that the spectators would have the sun behind them as they watched the fiddlers, the races, and the pulls. There were three buildings for animal exhibits. Horses and cows shared one. Pigs had another all to themselves. The third was reserved for "small animals," which included chickens, rabbits, game fowl, geese, and rodents of all kinds. Opposite the grandstand was a place to picnic. Those exhibiting pickles and vegetables sat at tables in the sun, with makeshift awnings and umbrellas to keep the contents of the jars from swelling until the glass containers burst with all the damage that an explosive might yield. Rumor had it that Jack Share's wandering eye was detached by a sliver of glass from just such an explosion, from a jar of pickled eggs. Naysayers claimed it just followed his wandering heart. Glass or heart, it made no difference. The wandering eye scared Lucy when she saw it. It saw her, too, and he laughed and pushed his face at her. It was a goofy laugh and it came out of a smile that sat sideways on his face and she wanted to point to her eggs but he touched her shoulder and all she could think about was Gwendolyn flying at the Hamburgs.

All of Homer turned out for the fair. There was an endless parade through the tents, and people paused at each table to admire the displays. Mrs. Wheeling sat to her right and showed her how to arrange her table to better display her eggs. This included tipping the plate ever so slightly. Lucy held her breath, afraid they would roll off, but the moss held them securely in place. She thanked Mrs. Wheeling just as she politely thanked the people who complimented her on her fine display. Her teacher, Miss Gesling, stopped to ask her about her summer, and whether she had given any consideration to learning how to play the piano. There was a scuffle at the other end of the tent, and Lucy heard Jack Share's goofy laugh and blustering voice and Miss Gesling assured her that it was of no concern of theirs and that they shouldn't even deign to look. Lucy liked that word, *deign,* and promised herself that she would share it with Maude when she got home. Miss Gesling wore the most beautiful green dress. She was like a willow tree, or like butter-and-eggs just before it blooms.

A man approached. He wore dark clothes, even in the heat. He muttered over her chickens and flashed Lucy a quick smile. A plume of smoke from his cigar followed his hand as he talked, a plume that circled and stabbed as he suddenly stuck it into her box. Lucy drew in her breath and nearly choked on the smoke. He jabbed his hand into her box! She stood, frozen, throat spasming at the shock of it. He thrust his hand into her box! He ruffled up Elizabeth, grabbed her by the legs, and lifted her into the air. Elizabeth protested. She flapped and fluttered and tried to peck at the man. He dropped her back in the box and leaned in, asking, conspiratorially, how much Lucy wanted. He smelled of blood and smoke and goats. Lucy, unable to breathe, shook her head, unable to answer. "Have your father contact Lou Verratio." It took several moments for Lucy to regain her breathing, moments she spent collecting Elizabeth's lost feathers. The cigar and its smoke moved about the small building, circling and jabbing, pausing over Mrs. Wheeling's Hamburgs and the Jersey Woolies brought by Mrs. Harnish, who giggled and blushed as he stroked her rabbits' ears and told her how beautiful they were compared to the Lops and Angoras. Mrs. Wheeling pouted and then turned to Lucy with a hushed voice to tell her she should wait. Verratio didn't give the best prices; Cooper and Sons gave better, as did Bedford. Bedford, she said, worked on the spot, which seemed an awful waste. He had to buy a winch to get the cows and pigs on the wagon afterwards. Cooper and Sons were smart enough to let them walk on by themselves. Verratio was not beyond stealing a horse or two to fill out his load, she said. Mrs. Harnish giggled. Mrs. Wheeling set herself straight in her chair. A horrid shudder shook Lucy as she began to realize what Mrs. Wheeling was talking about. She drew the boxes close and comforted her worried birds.

The problem of which chickens to take was slightly better the following year. In the interest of democratic participation, Winifred and Elizabeth couldn't go. That left Victoria, and the real choice between Catherine and Maude. She chose Catherine. In deference to Maude, she saved all of her eggs from the previous two weeks and displayed them. This year, she knew what to expect. This year, she breathed easier. She was able to protect her eggs from the jugglers and the boys who ran through the small-animal building. She was able to dodge the butchers and to protect Victoria and Catherine from their probing fingers by slipping them quickly under the table whenever she heard Mrs. Harnish giggle.

Her breath was stolen, however, when a young man set up a table across from hers and began wailing and crying. A crowd soon gathered. He hoisted a dead chicken into his lap and began plucking its feathers. He called out, "what in the world will save me from this mess! Oh drudgery! Oh, the fuss!" Feathers flew in all directions. His pants began to collect spots of blood and urine. His hands reddened with the work, and he rubbed his face where the blood mixed with his sweat. "Feathers and blood," he cried, "Havoc and ruin! When will it ever end!"

Suddenly, from the far end of the building, another voice cried out, "I can help you!" The crowd parted, dramatically. This second young man marched forward with something that looked like a seed spreader. Quicker than Lucy could sneeze, he produced another chicken and put it in his contraption. He spun a handle. Turned a crank. Feathers collected in a basket. He opened the lid, and pulled out the defeathered bird. The crowd applauded at the show. Lucy almost vomited. An hour later, the first young man set to wailing and crying. Another crowd began to gather, and Lucy hid under her table, talking softly to her birds, urging them through pursed lips not to look at the horror.

That year, Maude's eggs won first place.

• • •

A quick rise in the breeze and the smell of hay blows in through the window and fills the room. Lucy pauses at the sink. She has filled the barn with such a smell, filled it every year for years and years, a smell so pervasive that it filled her very pores. She has slept in the barn after the hay is in, just to fill herself with the smell. When she was small, when Ethel was alive, they lived in the barn for seven glorious days, burrowing through the bales like rats. It is the smell of the county fair, the horse and cow barn, the smell of June, late July, early September, summer.

Maude's eggs won first place. A blue ribbon for the blue eggs. A blue ribbon that earned her an invitation to bring those eggs and two chickens to the state fair. Lucy nearly screamed when Theodore Scruggs handed her the blue ribbon and an envelope containing the invitation. Mrs. Wheeling frumped and straightened her skirt. Mrs. Wheeling's Hamburgs frumped and fluffed their wings. Mrs. Harnish giggled.

The invitation came with a letter:

Dear Fowl Exhibitor,

Owing to the unsavory and unhealthy conditions of past fowl exhibits (including but not restricted to chickens, ducks, geese, guineas, partridges, peafowl, pigeons, pheasants, and turkeys), the State Board of Health now requires that all cages be fitted with rolling and disposable flooring. One design of such flooring can be found on the reverse of this notice. Alternately, exhibitors may opt to purchase from Burke's Farm and . . . .

The envelope included a three-page catalogue featuring Burke's products and an order form. Once Mrs. Wheeling unfrumped herself, she huffed at the letter. Once upon a time, she said, they let chickens run everywhere. Now, two cases of schistosomiasis and one of mad hen's disease and they bring in every whizz-bang and geegaw in the book. Mrs. Horn instructed her how best to display her birds: just before the judge arrives, she said, Lucy should ruffle their feathers and fan their feet. Mrs. Wheeling wheezed what sounded like a laugh. No, no, no, no, no, she said. Everyone knows that you have to dangle a cutworm before their eyes. It shows the judge their fire. Mrs. Harnish giggled. Mrs. Wheeling ruffled her skirt.

The design was at once ingenious and maddeningly infuriating. A roller filled with newsprint was affixed to one side of the cage. The paper was threaded *through* the bottom of the cage (not, the instructions made clear, *under* the cage) and over a second roller, whereupon it descended to a third, at which point the fouled paper was cut and discarded. The third roller sported a handle, which, when cranked, drew the paper through the cage, thereby providing a clean surface for the fowl to befoul. To Lucy, the entire apparatus looked altogether glorious and nothing less than what her blue ribbon Araucanas were due. The rollers would help keep their feet and feet feathers clean so that their colors might be fully appreciated by the judges and by the citizens of the entire state.

Lucy's father sat down with the letter and the design, and together they set about implementing her rolling and disposable flooring. Preparing the cage so that the paper would slide through was easy enough; her father took a pair of wire clippers and demonstrated how they would clip away the wires at the bottom. Then Lucy took over, carefully exerting all her strength against the wire. By the time she was done, her hands were sore and she had two blisters. They were "blue ribbon" blisters, Lucy proclaimed. She was decidedly satisfied with her work. Her father then took an old Homer *Ode* and slid it through the space Lucy had just cleared. Her job was uneven, however, and the paper caught and tore on the jagged bits of wire.

Then her father began to curse. First, there was the putting out. Everyone had to have a fancy system because a couple of people had not bothered to clean their birds' cages. Then there was the design itself. He could understand the changes they had just effected—the slot for sliding old newspapers through the bottom of the cage was a clever idea, and more than satisfied the health concerns (provided exhibitors bothered to change their newspapers on a regular basis). The roller system, however, was a mess. The more he looked at the primitive design, the more it stupefied him. Turning the handle would not move the paper through the cage, because the paper did not wrap around the third roller, the one with the handle. He puzzled and puzzled, and came to nothing. If the paper were to be taken up on that third roll, thereby allowing tension from the crank to draw the paper through the cage, the entire system would be rolling up the chickens' waste *in* the roll. This ran counter to the edict and to the design on the paper, which clearly indicated that the paper was to be torn off and thrown away. He cursed. Lucy clucked.

The picture in Burke's catalogue was deceptively drawn, twisted, angled, and otherwise impossible to discover how, with any precision, the system worked. Lucy's father cursed.

A night's sleep brought no illumination. Lucy grasped and pulled the paper through. The rollers spun. The handle sat immobile and useless. Lucy's father cursed.

A second night's sleep brought nightmares for father and daughter. Lucy dreamt that she was two inches small and chasing her chickens with a bucket as she tried to catch their poop. Her chickens, in turn, were chasing her, lovely grub that she was. The judges applauded their fired eyes, their ruffled feathers and fanned feet. Her father stood by, cursing. Mrs. Wheeler frumped. Mrs. Harnish giggled.

Her father dreamt that he set off for Rome behind his team but wound up in Homer, at Kesling's. He tried again and again, but all roads led to Homer. The vegetables on the wagon slowly turned to rot.

A week of fitful sleep brought no resolution. Her father gave up, flummoxed and befuddled by the madness. The cursing stopped. In all her sixty years, Lucy never went to the state fair. She sets Hester's egg on the counter to her right, freshly washed and glowing.

•   •   •

Ethel's mother died when Ethel and Lucy were eight. She died in the summer, when the hay was cut and drying in the fields, when Ethel's father was logging in the north, when Ethel herself was playing catch-as-catch-can with Lucy in the field behind Lucy's chicken coop. Ethel had come to stay with Lucy for two weeks while her mother suffered the final stages of her confinement. Lucy recognized the deep and underlying tremors that ran through her friend as Ethel's father delivered her to the care of Lucy and her parents. Ethel stood in the yard, fighting back a tear and struggling with a small valise. She lost both battles. The tear slowly made its way down her cheek; the valise dropped without ceremony to the grass at her feet.

Lucy, however, could barely contain her joy. It was all she could do not to streak across the yard to her friend, not to grab her by the hand and dance her to the chicken coop, not to hold up each bird and display its feathers, its wattles, its comb, and the fiery dash of gold in its eye. It was all she could do not to race her friend about the yard with a burst of giggling skips and jumps. It was all she could do not to drag her up the stairs to her room where she would show Ethel her marvelous survey of her world—the yard and the coop, the fields, the tree line, and the creek that it marked. It was all she could do not to burst out of her skin as she stood, half-listening to Ethel's father and watching the sole tear move with such precision down her friend's cheek. The dropping of the valise was like the dropping of the flag at the fairgrounds—and like the horses—she bolted. She covered the ground from the door to her friend like a quarter horse, and stopped just as quickly.

Ethel's gaze met her own. The tear already drying in the afternoon sun, her dark hair striking against the colors of summer, her blue eyes penetrating Lucy's brown, her lower lip on the edge of a quiver.

"Oh Lucy!" she gushed and leapt forward. Ethel's arms wrapped tightly around Lucy, who returned the embrace. "Oh Ethel," she whispered.

For a full week they commanded all that was Lucy's world.

They ran everywhere they went. From the house to the chicken coop, a thunder of feet. Lucy showed Ethel her chickens: Victoria, Catherine, Elizabeth, Winifred, and Maude. Ethel did what Lucy dared not, or dared not say aloud—she immediately selected a favorite from the flock. Drawn by the red-tips in the bird's cheek feathers, Ethel chose Catherine. She hoisted her from the floor of the coop, pulled her into her lap, and stroked the chicken's beak with her thumb. Catherine cocked her head and panted, her lower beak dropping for a better scent. Ethel's dress fell about her, a calico backdrop. The soft strokings mesmerized Lucy, but the rest of her birds twisted and primped on the roost with enough fuss to break the spell. Each morning, while Ethel stroked Catherine, Lucy calmed the rest of the flock, reminding them all how special they were as she collected their eggs.

Ethel gushed over the soft blue eggs, and helped Lucy wash them at the kitchen sink. Lucy's hands pause at that distant memory—four hands rinsing eggs, small hands, interchangeable hands, indistinguishable hands, busy hands—they can still recall Ethel's laughing touch as they nearly dropped an egg.

They pretended they were chickens and raced about the yard, their arms on the rise, their dresses fluffed and full. They met, as

the young chicks met, testing themselves against each other—
running and running until they jumped, chests crashing together,
and collapsed in the grass into a fit of giggles.

Each day, they waded the creek, their dresses held high above
their knees, their shoes abandoned on the bank, their feet sinking
in the soft mud. Once, Lucy felt the mud move beneath her toes, a
frog, she hoped, and hopped out of the creek, the mud releasing
her with a sucking smack. Ethel laughed and pretended she was
a swan, gliding through the waters, looking for frogs to eat. Lucy
hopped about, dodging the darting snaps of Ethel's beak. They
drank the creek water and forgot the rest of the world as they lay
on their backs on the bank playing the memory game. They
laughed so long that their dresses dried, so loud that the swallows
swooped in from the barn to see the commotion.

At night, they watched the moon make its way across the window. They talked about their teacher and storytelling hour, and
about their favorite candies from Sunderson's confectionery.
Ethel preferred licorice. She loved licorice in any form. Lucy
loathed licorice, or so she said, because it sounded wonderful to
say such a thing in the dark. Her face hurt from smiling.

"I've been to the cemetery at night," whispered Ethel as a cloud
drifted across the moon's face. Lucy's smile disappeared. Her eyes
rounded in the dark. Her heart stopped.

"Did you hear?"

"Yes," said Lucy, a hushed exhale that allowed her heart to
begin beating again.

"Do you know what I saw?"

Lucy didn't know what to say. She had never thought about
cemeteries, or ghosts, or nocturnal meanderings, but suddenly,
she found herself afraid to speak.

"Miss Gesling." Ethel lay still in the dark.

Lucy was afraid to move. Miss Gesling? She couldn't imagine
her teacher outside their classroom. Miss Gesling was forever

standing in the front with her hair coiled behind her, her eyes soft and kind as they fell upon her, upon Ethel, upon the rest of the girls—eyes that hardened at the merest movement from the boys.

"What was she doing?" whispered Lucy.

Ethel lay still in the dark. The cloud continued to move across the moon's face, leaving Ethel a dim gray specter. As the moon reappeared, she glowed in the night, her white nightgown reflecting the moon's light.

"Putting daisies on her sister's grave."

Lucy was so distracted by Ethel's ghostly appearance that it took her a moment to envision her teacher walking about the cemetery, daisies in hand.

Then they were outside, picking toadflax, gliding about the night in their nightgowns in search of the small grave Lucy had made for Gwendolyn. They inhaled the rich scent of the flowers and Ethel laid hers over the rocks Lucy had placed over her hen. In the coop, Maude ruffled herself on the roost before settling back to sleep. It startled Ethel, startled her so much that she stifled a scream. Temperance snorted. Chastity raised a foot and set it down, her hoof scraping the stall on its way. Ethel stifled a second scream. Lucy laughed. Ethel pouted in the moonlight. Night sounds.

Then a soft scrumbling, a most unhen-like scrumbling from the chicken coop. Lucy's heart froze. Ethel hadn't heard and was beginning to hum, a petulant hum meant to ignore her friend. Lucy shushed her. Ethel shushed back. Lucy shushed. Ethel shushed. Lucy. Ethel. Lucy hissed. Ethel heard the scrumbling.

"Stop scaring me," she said.

Lucy strained against the rest of the night, strained her ears against the horses chewing in the barn, the rhythmic calling of the bullfrogs, the breeze through the leaves. The scrumbling was coming from the chicken coop. She inched forward, flowers clenched in her whitened fist, her other hand reaching for the latch on the door. Inside, Elizabeth issued a low chuckling cluck, as if to welcome the girl. Lucy lifted the latch and opened the door a crack—a crack too much. The sound of the hinges, the sudden extra light from the moon, the racing of her heart, one or some combination thereof startled the animal that had been rooting around the floor, and it swung around, not to face her, as she might have expected, but to turn away, tail to the young girl, tail raised . . .

Lucy slammed shut the door and ran, stifling her own scream along the way.

"Lucille Charlotte Barton Delano!" stomped her friend. "Stop scaring me this instant!"

Lucy stopped and turned, just as the situation dawned on Ethel.

"Skunk!" they screamed, in unison, and ran around to the front of the house, to the safety of the front porch, while the chicken coop filled with the frightened glands of the black and white animal.

They huddled together on the porch, whispering and giggling, as the night air caught the scent.

The skunk escaped the coop and ambled by the giggling girls, across the road, and into the field.

Victoria, Catherine, Elizabeth, Winifred, and Maude blinked and teared in the acrid odor, trapped on their roost, trapped with the smell.

•   •   •

The sound of an engine, two cylinders firing, two missing, a searing, jagged commotion. The sound rises and fades, followed by a whirl of dust that surrounds the house. It hangs in the air, laced with smoke, black smoke from the errant cylinders. Her nose wrinkles at the smell and she hesitates half a moment before closing the window. Elias Bligh. Three eggs dried on a towel next to the sink.

2

Sunday, Aug. 14, 1887 Warm 3 eggs Cece is brooding, not mixing w/other hens
Harold came with news of the accident.

Harold would run as fast as he could, run through the fields just for the running of it, outrunning the deerflies and the horseflies, outrunning all of the biting creatures, becoming the wind each time his feet left the ground. He would have loved to have driven an automobile, would have loved the speed of it. Even more, he would have loved piloting an airplane, had either machination been handy. Instead, he would run, fast and out of control, to the edge of tumbling head over heels, to the edge of the world.

He was running because the doctor looked up, spotted him in the crowd, and told him to. He was running flat out because the doctor held him by the ears and told him to. No one ever told him to stop, nor did stopping ever cross his mind. He came on, running for all he was worth, his legs churning through the hayfield, his lungs blowing out though his mouth. He pressed on, in the final five hundred yards of a five-mile sprint, 'til he stumbled up the porch where Lucy stood, as though he had crossed the finish line as he crossed into the yard proper, and let his body go, rag doll, stumbling, tumbling onto the porch. All his speed, all his extra effort was somewhat ill-spent, as it took him a full five minutes to regain his breath before he could speak, five minutes that Lucy used to get him a quart of water and to stand, waiting for him, feeling the faint odor of sweat permeate the air, healthy sweat, she thought, subliminally, good sweat. . . . She inhaled, deeply, breathing in to the depths of her soul, even as she refused to let the smell, let alone such thoughts, bubble to the surface.

She inhaled deeply when he finally got his wind and sputtered something about an accident . . . her parents . . . the doctor . . . running to tell her. . . . He had refused the road and saved a mile. His hair was pasted to his forehead and darker for the sweat. An accident. Number 289, the train to Utica, had unhooked a refrigerator car at the ice plant, and the car had tipped, spilling its entire contents on the street. They had been buried by the ice. No one saw them, no one knew they were buried under the tons of crystallized water until it melted enough for the brakeman to spot her mother's parasol.

She fell back, disbelieving, *her* air now gone, punched out of her. Harold's own breathing began to settle into a more regular, less dramatic heaving of his ribs. He was about to say more, to tell her about the doctor, his arrival after the accident, his attempts to revive them, first her mother, then her father, but their lives had left them, left their cold and senseless bodies. He was about to tell her of the crowd that gathered, and how they looked on, providing their own eulogies at the scene, recognizing her father for the cleanliness with which he kept the farm, her mother for her good deeds, and speculating what would come of the farm now that they were gone, almost forgetting Lucy as their thoughts forged ahead. He could have told her how Hank Anfall and George Waters and Lemon Fink and Frank Harmon joked that the farm could be had for the wooing of Lucy, but that the price was too steep. They punched each other as part of the fun and then began throwing ice at each other until the sheriff intervened. The doctor announced there was nothing he could do, and singled Harold out for the unpleasant duty of telling Lucy the news. The boys snickered and made kissing noises as Harold lit out down the street. They were minor nuisances compared to the deerflies and brambles he fought on the way. So, he came on, running for all he was worth, until he arrived, spent.

Her swoon, or the hint of one that came from the smell of his sweat, suddenly became real as her air left her.

With her collapse, he leapt to his feet, his energy suddenly returned. He picked up the jar, raced to the pump for water, and returned to empty its contents in her face. He never told her the details. Not then, not ever.

•   •   •

Lucy stands at her kitchen sink, clutching the counter with the memory. He had run five miles, through the fields and woods, crossing the creek twice, to tell her. Now, she finds herself desperate to know how they died, as though the entire world hangs on the answer. Were they crushed? Had they frozen to death? Were they smothered, or drowned?

Their deaths were intimately wrapped up with the smell of him, of sweat, of the pollen that clung to his clothing, of the muck of the creeks. He guzzled the water she brought him and set the jar on the porch. It was a quart jar. She wonders, idly, which jar it might be amidst the twenty or more that grace the shelves in the pantry, or if there is any way to tell. Most contain tomatoes she canned the previous summer, but there are two that hold pickled eggs, suspiciously old, a failed experiment. She can't remember when she spent an afternoon doing such a thing, and she is afraid of opening either jar. She makes a note to do so soon.

Lucy wets a cloth and wipes her face. Five fresh eggs sit on the counter to her left, ready to be washed, flecks of dirt on their shells. She can almost imagine the route he took as he left town, the burden of bad tidings urging him on. He would have followed the road for a good mile, passing the Gouldens and the Lamarques before striking out through Rice's cow pasture. That stretch of ground was so filled with rocks that it was unplowable and good for nothing but grazing. She picks up an egg, clearly Hannah Hoes's from the tapered end, and runs it under the water. The Rices had Devons at the time, perhaps a dozen or more. They would have hardly lifted their heads though he would have run right through their midst. The horses in the Cranes' pasture would have bolted at the first sound of him—more quickly than the deer, who would have waited until he came into sight and stomped their forelegs once or twice before bounding away. But the Thoroughbreds, Seth Crane's pride and joy, would have flown away with his puffing. Harold would have had to cross the creek there, after the fence. She imagines him leaping over it, though it was more likely that he'd thrown himself on the ground and rolled under the lowest board. The creek wasn't more than knee-deep, though it was wide enough to soak him. She scratches at the dirt that clings to Jacqueline's egg, dipping it into the water three times before the dirt loosens itself from the shell. She always wondered how her hens managed to get so much dirt into their nest boxes. The boxes are ready for a cleaning.

Mary Ellen's egg had come out soft and had hardened in the nest. It is ever so slightly flattened on one side. Curious, Lucy thinks, as she sets it on the towel; it does not roll to the flattened side.

The creek water would have been warm in August, though not as warm as the air that day. Had he crossed at night, the temperatures might have been reversed. Later that summer, she and Harold swam, together, late at night and marveled at the phenomenon; it was almost like taking a warm bath in running water, but only because the air felt so cool when they emerged under the August moon. Had he not been so charged with delivering the news, he might have paused at the creek for a drink, but he waited for that relief. Nor was it the best spot to be drinking, since the creek swung round and into Rice's cow pasture. The cows often stood in the water, cooling their udders, emptying their bladders and colons. The water grew foul at times. Positively foul.

From the creek, it would have been a full mile through the trees and low scrub that divided Rice's farm from Westers'. The Moultons lived there now, having cleared the scrub and two acres of ground for the house and gardens around the turn of the century. There is a phrase she hasn't thought about in years. Harold used it often, planning big things by "the turn of the century." More than a dozen years before such turning, he was talking big, wishing instead it were "the end of the millennium," or, rather, "the beginning of a new millennium," or, better, "the turn of the millennium" on the horizon. But he told her that he would have to be satisfied with the beginning of a new century. How many people got a chance at such a renewal?! Lucy thought the number must be quite large, but hadn't said so at the time. When the century had finally turned, she almost missed it. If it hadn't been for her egg diary, she would have.

The low scrub would have slowed Harold slightly on his race to her. He might have scared a turkey hen and her poults—that was where they collected in the summers, before the Moultons began clearing the low growth. Sometimes there were as many as fifty turkeys, preening and cooing. She had snuck down there with Ethel one day and watched them for hours. The poults, in flocks of ten or more, spread their wings, testing them, sending their bodies out of control—up in the air and down, ten or twenty of them bouncing through the underbrush. The sight knocked them silly. She and Ethel flapped and bounced and jumped and flounced and scared the birds so much that they ran around and around, their heads alone straining upward over the grasses and shrubs to see what the girls were about. If Harold scared them, it would have been for little more than a moment as he flew over the ground, bounding over shrubs like the little birds themselves.

The creek on the other side would have been more of the same, but the Westers had thrown several large rocks into the water, rocks that served as stepping stones. The stones collected sticks and twigs and leaves so much that they almost worked as a small dam. As a result a small pool formed, where minnows rested and where it was rumored a granddaddy catfish lived. Catfish didn't get to be granddaddies without eating, and this one had eaten everything: minnows, trout, the old gray snapper, a small dog, and the foot off one of the Crandall girls. She'd gone away from the shame of it, moved to California, to San Francisco, where misfits and gold diggers of all kinds congregated in the misfit capital of the world. She couldn't write, so no one ever heard from her again. Ethel and Lucy had been careful not to put their feet in the water there, careful not to make a sound for fear of attracting Daddy Catfish as they crossed. Harold must have stayed on the rocks.

She dips an egg in the water and rubs it as Harold runs the Westers' back woods. They are glorious woods, birches giving way to maples, old maples, nearly as old as the granddaddy catfish, but kind. In the fall, she had sat in those woods when the breeze came up and released hundreds upon hundreds of whirling maple seeds. Harold's run would have been slowed by the closeness of the birches, but he would have gained speed through the maples. Their branches are surprisingly high as they stretch for the sun. Her fingers linger over the egg's surface, almost caressing it in the warm water. Nelly's is textured, like the fields with their rocks emerging through the soil.

She can see him coming on, straight-lined through the tall grass that was ready for haying, ignoring the paths carved through it by the deer, who traveled the field each night.

She can see him coming on, the tall grass parting with his passing, egg warm and smooth in her hand.

She can see him coming on through the field, his arms pumping, his hair flying.

She can see him coming on, and she feels the warm crumble of shell and the viscous flow of yolk and albumen through her fingers as they close tight around Abigail Childress's egg.

. . .

Saturday, Oct. 15, 1887 Seasonably cool 5 eggs Pearl is depressed Shortbread has the hiccups All of their feathers are a bit scruffy

Clear sky, but thunder all morning! Oh Ethel!

Lucy looks to her hands, the yolk mixing with the albumen, obscuring the lines, so many lines, filling their depths. Her fingers curl naturally in toward the palms, the cut on the index finger of her left hand is nearly healed. Her pinkies bend inward. The yellow yolk has sent out flares toward her thumb.

They'd played with the eggs, with bits of cloth, making hats and dresses and shirts and tresses and naming them—this one, with bits of black cloth, was the mayor and he barked and barked like the Rices' old dog who barked at everything from the horse and carriage that passed on by, to the tired or stupid June bugs that bounced against the house in the late afternoon. This one was Mizzus Waring, who took the boys to the woodshed and made them drop their pants and took the switch to them. She never took the girls, even when Melody Hinkle spilled an entire bottle of ink and accidentally stepped in it, making black, smeary footprints all over the classroom when she ran out, crying. This one was Miss Gesling with her wisps of hair that escaped everywhere, always on the edge of wild abandon. She walked about the classroom one day with a garter snake in her hands. Its tongue darted at them as she pushed it into their faces. She came to Lucy.

"What does it feel like, Lucy?" she asked.

Lucy squirmed in her seat. Her skirt fluffed and ruffled and her hands tried to smooth it.

"Slimy."

"Touch it, Lucy," she said, pushing the snake closer. "Touch the snake."

It took a moment. Her hand stopped of its own accord on its way to the scaled beast, and she had to will it the rest of the way. Two fingers darted out and made quick contact, and just as quickly retreated.

"Touch it, Lucy," Miss Gesling said. Softer now. Wisps dangling in front of her eyes.

She touched it, stroked it, stroked it again.

"What does it feel like?"

It was rough. Scratchy. Dry. Not slimy at all.

Ethel danced Miss Gesling her way, a bit of wild grass hanging in her face.

"Oh Lucy, please write one hundred more sentences on the board."

Lucy quickly picked up Garnar Rischel.

"Ooh, ooh, let me! Let me! I want to write sentences on the board!"

"Oh Ir-ma. Ir-maaa." Suddenly, Mr. Sunderson appeared in Ethel's left hand. "I have something sweet for you!"

Ethel danced Mr. Sunderson and Miss Gesling toward each other, and Lucy watched, horrified.

"Something sweet?"

"Just for you."

"Just for me?"

And they were smacking their lips as Ethel brought them together. Kissing. Miss Gesling cracked. Egg white seeped out, wetting the bits of grassy wisps and pasting them to her head.

John Gorman kissed Ethel when she turned eleven. They had a birthday party for her at school, and John embarrassed himself by puckering up and launching a kiss that might have been special. But he caught her in the eye, and she jumped back, in startled pain. John's emboldenment was temporary. He had screwed up enough courage to kiss her, but he had forgotten the torment that would follow. It followed. It took him two years to gather enough courage to try again. This time, he waited until they were alone, walking. This time his aim was better. This time, she was ready for it, and helped his aim. Their lips met. She later reported to Lucy that it had been nice. That a boy's lips weren't slimy at all. That they were rough. A little scratchy. A little dry. But definitely not slimy. A little later, Ethel worried that she wasn't very good at kissing.

Lucy rubs her hands together, thoroughly mixing the white and yolk. They aren't slimy. They are slightly viscous, slightly sticky, and don't mix well with the water when she dips her hands into the sink to rinse them. It has taken all those years to see what she had known all along. She exhales slowly through her nose. She hears the tractor firing down the road.

•   •   •

Ethel did not die of a broken heart. To hear some people, a body would have thought that as soon as Gorman left town, she pined away to nothing. Nothing could have been further from the truth. Anyone with half a brain would have known that Gorman had left town three years before she died. He'd gone to Albany and began working for a haberdasher. "Life is grand," he'd written. "I have a hat on my head and a stick in my hand, and, so outfitted, I parade State Street and Grand Street where the state's best show off their finery."

"Albany!" exclaimed Ethel.

Lucy didn't know what to say and picked at a few loose strands of her shawl. Her worst fear was that Ethel would go to Albany to join Gorman, and that she would never see her friend again.

"Albany!" exclaimed Ethel, again, when Lucy remained silent.

They were eating their dinners in the park. It was early summer. Lucy had come to town to deliver the farm's production to the merchants and wholesalers, but also to spend a couple of hours with her friend.

"Albany!" she exclaimed for the third time. "Why stop in Albany!"

Ethel's face was flushed. Her eyes were animated and saw beyond Homer, beyond Albany to the world. She turned, suddenly, to Lucy.

"Do you know what I read? They are having a World Fair in Paris! They're building a tower and inviting people from India and Africa and South America. Even people from China! Imagine, the entire world at the fair!"

Lucy was imagining. She was already caught up in the small-animal display—it would be marvelous, she thought, with hundreds and hundreds of chickens. There would be Cochins and Crevecoeurs and Malays and Anconas. She could hear Mrs. Harnish giggling in French, then Spanish, then Chinese.

Lucy began to flush.

Ethel raced on.

"Do you know what I am thinking?" she asked. "I'm thinking we should go! We should go to the World Fair! Oh, it will be wonderful! We'll go to New York and take a steamer to Calais. Then we will travel by train to Paris. Oh, it will be wonderful!"

•   •   •

The very next Friday, Ethel had news.

"I have a job!" She nearly screamed with joy. "I have a job! We'll save and save and save until we can go to Paris!" Ethel had become a secretary for Peter Estranger Nixy, former mayor of Homer.

Such were their Friday dinners through that winter. Lucy began to catch Ethel's excitement. She imagined New York. She imagined the steamer. She imagined the train to Paris. She imagined Paris and the World Fair and the Tower of Babel. She imagined Ethel dancing through the streets of New York, in the ballroom on the steamer, in Paris itself. . . . She imagined Ethel smiling, her teeth, her face catching the sun, the French sun!

Lucy flushed with the excitement.

But for all of her excitement, for all of her imagining, for all of her trying, she could not imagine *herself* in any of those scenes. It was too much, too big, too scary, too . . . too . . . too . . . much of something that was beyond her imagination.

Still, she flushed.

By January, her eggs had earned her enough material to begin sewing a travel dress.

.   .   .

By the end of winter, Lucy completed four dresses suitable for travel. She also completed two parasols: one for herself and the other for Ethel, made from layers upon layers of cheesecloth and dyed with walnuts and berries. She took them with her to town one warm Friday in early April on a day that the sun shown hard and bright. The snow had melted and the streets were mud, but the park was perfect for walking. She presented Ethel with her parasol. Ethel clapped her hands together. They were perfect! she exclaimed. She loved the burst of colors, of reds and yellows, that ran through them. She loved the cheesecloth, the willow and ash. She held it up against the sun and marveled at it from the inside. It was difficult for Lucy not to burst with her own joy.

"Let's walk," she said.

They strolled the park, kindly nodding to one passerby after the next, twirling their parasols over their shoulders this way and that—two swirls of bright colors against the mud and brick and pale blue sky. Ethel affected a British accent.

"Napoleon was a bit of a rake," she said. "Don't you think?"

Lucy paused the swirling of her parasol without missing a step.

"A bit of a rake?" she said. "More like the entire toolshed."

She didn't quite know what she meant by it, but it sounded divine, and Ethel agreed.

"Look there," Ethel pointed, with her nose. "I believe that is the Emperor of Japan. He looks well today."

"As well as can be expected," said Lucy. "All things considered."

"Yes," said Ethel, "and one always must consider all things."

"The Empress is a delight," said Lucy, her parasol spinning now clockwise, now counterclockwise.

"If you say so, dear," said Ethel.

So they strolled the park, kindly greeting the world.

So they strolled on Fridays, through April and May, and into the summer months. Their parasols bloomed with the spring and carried the dashes of color through August. On their walks, they met the King of England, ivory merchants, gold barons, and countless counts and countesses. They stepped and twirled and strolled and whirled their summer away.

Then came Harold's run.

Then came Harold's run.

Lucy's parasol sat in the corner of the kitchen. She had been working on two hats—the felt and netting and thread lay untouched on the table in the parlor. She received visits from her neighbors: kind words, a bushel of apples, cordwood, promises for the fall. She fed the horses and mucked their stalls. Their familiar breathing, their quiet stomping of flies, the smell of their sweat was comforting. She received visits from her neighbors: kind wishes, hot dishes, pledges for the winter. She fed the dowdy Hamburgs and collected their eggs. She received a visit from Harold on Sunday. He sat quietly while she grieved, and offered to clean the harnesses. She fed her Araucanas. They gathered around her as she sobbed. They cooed and warbled their concern, and pecked at the fringe of her dress. She received visits from bankers and speculators, fat with cigars. Sell, they said. They tromped about the property uninvited, inspecting the conditions of the barns and outbuildings, the roof, the fields, the yards, the wells. They stalked the perimeter of the house, peering in the windows, knocking on the walls. Lucy's breathing grew shallow. They waved papers with numbers on them—offers on the farm. In the shuffling sound of the papers she thought she heard Mrs. Harnish giggle. Suddenly, Jack Share's rolling eye filled her vision and she screamed. In the barn, Temperance snorted. Chastity raised a foot and set it down, her hoof scraping the stall on its way.

On Friday, she harnessed Temperance and Chastity and went to town with the farm's weekly production, greatly reduced. She took an hour to walk with Ethel. She felt drained, as though there were no tears left. She told Ethel everything. About the neighbors and Harold and the bankers. About the apples and cordwood. About the promises and pledges. About the shuffling sound of papers and Mrs. Harnish's giggle. About the emptiness that was everywhere. She found more tears.

"Besides," she cried, "where would I live?"

"Oh Lucy!" Ethel wrapped her arms around her. "You can live with me!"

Lucy sat at the center of a deep black hole. The reins were loose in her hands; the horses knew the way. When they turned into the yard, she suddenly snapped out of her trance. Her Araucanas raced about the yard chasing mosquitoes, invisible in the late afternoon. They leapt and lunged at the air. They popped and swirled. They tumbled and turned. They fluffed their wings. They stretched their heads higher and higher. Their eyes swiveled. They were crazy streaks of colors and snapping beaks. They looked positively mad.

· · ·

Ethel did not die of a broken heart. She died of a curious conjunction of circumstances. Standing at the sink with her hands

covered with egg, Lucy begins to think the circumstances somewhat less curious and somewhat more suspicious. Peter Estranger Nixy, affectionately called P.U. by those who benefited
from his generosity, had used his power as mayor to bring into his
possession three saloons, twenty-three buildings that he rented
to businesses and families alike, the funeral home, and the cemetery—this was P.U.'s world. This was his kingdom. It was a kingdom, he liked to say, that stretched as far as the eye could see.

Lucy scans her world from her kitchen window and is surprised at how little the eye can see, thankful, too, for the stand of
trees she planted and for how much less she saw. She stands, still
and silent in a house filled with creaking and snaps.

Nixy thought that his citizens might benefit from his autobiog-
raphy and hired Ethel as a secretary. Her principal responsibility
was to take dictation as he lounged about his office, erupting into
one memory after another, interrupted by a steady stream of toad-
ies. Ethel worked hard to learn the stenograph; its keys were a
baffling array of confusions that she mastered by thinking of
something else. She was at once lost in thought and busily record-
ing her employer's first mayoral campaign when a telegram arrived. He continued to talk, Ethel typed madly to keep up, reached
back, stretching to meet the hand of the telegraph boy, her right
hand missing a whole series of strokes, while her left hand continued, unconsciously, as if the right were still tapping away. History
was lost in the eighteen seconds it took to receive the telegram,
and, in those eighteen seconds, history extracted its revenge.
Major John Colter of the Homer Militia, a militia that had given
distinguished service in battles both for and against the union of
states, chose at that awkward moment to test its newest battery.
Ethel was oblivious to the cascade of books that buried her in
their collective weight of history, a cascade precipitating from
Major John's concussive blast loosed some two miles away, a
blast that sent a sonic shiver through Homer, shaking and rat-

tling the town, and breaking the uppermost shelving of a wall-size bookcase until down they came, one shelf after another, a series of hapless jolts until Ethel, poor Ethel, lay buried by history.

•   •   •

When Lucy buried her parents, she followed immediately behind the casket leading a long line of mourners, from friends and neighbors to her parents' cousins and other distant members of the family. They turned off Market Street into "Haskins," the unofficial name of the town's main cemetery, took an immediate left, and processed past Heywood, Haskins, and Grambly until they arrived at the Delanos' small plot, tucked up against two evergreens. Two mounds of dirt marked the tragedy. Ethel stood by her side as a few kind words caught the wind, swirled and rose, ascendant. The mourners filed past. Lucy had declined a viewing, so they took this opportunity to pay their respects and offer Lucy their condolences. She noticed with a numb curiosity that Christine Crébillon stretched her hand out to touch her mother's casket. It was a singular touch.

When Ethel was buried, Lucy wore one of her travel dresses; she was ushering her friend to a better world. She heard fish splashing and a distant cry of a baby as she followed a short line of mourners. They turned off Market Street, into the cemetery and to the right. The gravel path led around to the back toward the river, where a single mound of dirt awaited. The grass there was longer, infused with toadflax and wood vetch, and there were a considerable number of trees, more hemlock than the oak and evergreens that had been planted elsewhere. At the time, Lucy was surprised at Ethel's final resting site, but only because it was so far from her own parents'. Only after several years of walking back and forth across the cemetery to pay her respects did she discover the town's history in its headstones. Each Friday, she would exchange her eggs and baskets and hay, or vegetables, or grains. Then she would spend an hour or two walking through the trees amongst the stones. During those hours, the muscles in her face would soften and her eyes would grow round. The tears dried after the first year.

On these Fridays, Lucy learned more history than Miss Gesling ever knew, history that was beyond Nixy's imagination. Ethel was buried a stone's throw from Marie LeFleur. The infamous LeFleur's headstone, however, simply had her first name, Marie, d1753. Marie was a combination of French and Mohawk. History had it that she married Racine LeFleur after the Frenchman escaped (deserted) the French army and settled outside what was to become Homer proper. When those first three families—Heywood, Haskins, and Grambly—set their shovels at the confluence of two muddy creeks, when they then claimed enough land so that they might sell lots to a storekeeper, a cooper, and a blacksmith, Marie escaped her husband to work in the store. She was vilified by the English Protestants, who were certain she was a witch. Her death, the town's first, gave them a problem: what to do with the body. The suggestions were numerous and included floating her down the creek. In the end, they dragged her body a half mile away and dug a shallow grave. No one knows who placed the stone that honored her, but it appeared the following year. No one knows who modified it, carving the mark of Wicca into the stone soon after. The tracks that led to the LeFleur homestead were less than helpful. No one at that residence had the skill to effect such a mark.

The shade was cooling in the heat of August and made Lucy's Friday afternoon walks pleasant. Her travel dresses grew more comfortable with the years, and her parasol spun in the sun. She became acquainted with the women in the area surrounding Marie's grave: Nelly Waters, Jacqueline LaForche, Mary Ellen Worthington, Sarah Levine, Hannah Hoes, Abigail Childress. She memorized their names and told Ethel stories about them, stories that Ethel already knew, no doubt. Nelly grew up to be a schoolteacher and taught two generations of the town's youth before passing on. Jacqueline LaForche was spurned in love; the youngest Haskins son left her at the altar. She had her revenge through the years by slowly poisoning his yard with purple nightshade. Mary Ellen Worthington would have become a member of the town council had she lived long enough. Lucy sighed with the tragedies she suffered; a stillborn, a rakish man, a bout with scabies, and through it all, she remained beloved, until she died. Sarah Levine was the first woman to own a business—a dressmaker's shop. But she didn't pay enough attention to the husbands. She doted on the ladies, doted on the wives and daughters, and slowly went out of business and out of favor. Sarah died a pauper. Hannah Hoes became the wife of a president. A whirlwind of a courtship and she was off to the White House. But she slowly went insane and was locked away in the pink room, away from the public, away from home. Abigail Childress lived alone in a small house on the edge of town. When the railroad came through, they wanted to run the tracks through her house. Abigail refused to leave. The town threatened her. "Never," she cried. "I will never leave my house." The town generously made the fuse to the dynamite stretch across the street to give Abigail enough time to leave. "Never," she cried as they lit the fuse. "Never," she cried as her house exploded. She still haunted the town, crying "Never" whenever a train came through.

One winter, Lucy was surprised to stumble across Alice Haskins, granddaughter to the great man. The summer weeds, thistle and vetch, had hidden her gravestone. But in the stark white of winter, she discovered Alice, banished from the Haskins family plots. Up to then, Lucy had thought that she had been wandering the paupers' graves, and that the mark was the mark of the poor, not a mark of Wicca, but the discovery of Alice Haskins changed all that. She never did come to another explanation for the mark, lost as she was in the details of the stones, the paths, the flowers and trees.

The cemetery was not without humor. After a time, Lucy was able to come to it with a smile. Longtime typesetter for the Homer *Ode,* Hiram Putnam's stone had the following:

May he rest with ease.

The back of his stone was covered with e's. Lowercase e's. Upper-case e's. Italicized e's. E's of all sizes and fonts. One e for every e he lost as he set type at his darkened table.

The mason had carved Zeigfried Anfall's stone into a profile of the distinguished man, or, rather distinguished the stone by depicting him in profile—and celebrating his enormous nose. Lucy almost laughed out loud when she came across the Anfall plots. Noses proliferated. They protruded from the faces of the stones, from the sides of the stones, even from the tops of the stones. One year, someone planted tulips under each Anfall nose. The flowers grew and blossomed. Lucy wondered if the mystery planter knew that the Anfalls typically suffered hay fever.

Lucy stifles a sneeze. Ethel's heart was never broken.

•　　•　　•

Sunday, Jan. 1, 1888 Cold No eggs Enid and Bernice look very funny
　　Creek froze.

Harold arrived with the New Year, and with as much promise and vim as a body might wish, given the expanse that lay before them, and a Leap Year, too!

He positively sparkled, much like the sun off the snow. Lucy found it difficult to look at him, so blindingly bright was he. She shook, and shook again, shaking off the old year, looking forward to the promise, the promises of the new. She had spent the New

Year's Eve in the dark, thinking about her parents, about Ethel, about something she had no words for.

Harold paced the kitchen, fully energized with the cold. His energy filled the room and enlivened her.

"How about an eggnog?" he said. "To celebrate the future!"

There were no fresh eggs. Lucy had to use the ones laid the day before by Martha Wayles, Lucretia, Dolley, and Mary Todd. She broke them over a bowl and set the shells to one side. She added a bit of milk and a bit of brandy. Harold added a bit more brandy, laughed, and yet a bit more. She whisked the mixture, catching his laughter and returning her own. She whisked it into a froth and poured it into two tall glasses.

Harold toasted the new year.

Harold toasted Lucy.

Harold toasted the two of them.

Then, with the glow of the brandy just beginning to fire, he proposed.

Just like that.

He proposed.

•   •   •

Just like that. He proposed. She laughed and said yes without thinking, caught by the joy of it, by the promise of it. She laughs again, now, at the thought of it. Her Sundays with Harold had ripened into a frothy eggnog and an engagement. A winter engagement. Harold wanted to get married on Leap Day, to take a leap (as if they hadn't leapt into the new year), as he put it, not just a step, not a hop, not a skip, not a jump, but a leap into each other's futures. But the pastor refused to marry anyone on a Thursday, and his schedule was full until March 11th. Harold moped at the delay. Lucy pursed her lips and thought him silly.

Two weeks were not enough to silence Emma Grambly, who

thought anything less than a year was unseemly. Emma made certain that she was in Kesling's on Fridays when Lucy arrived flush with eggs. Emma's comments were loud and frequent: the lack of a chaperone during her Sundays with Harold would earn Lucy eternal damnation. Kesling nodded and harumpfed as he counted the soft blue eggs and tallied them in his book. Satyrine, she hissed through a broken tooth. Temptress. Lucy's shoulders stiffened under the steady stream of invectives. Emma was relentless. Kesling nodded and harumpfed.

Lucy did not mourn Emma's passing and surprised herself when she toasted her death with an eggnog. Lucy barely recognized her twinge of guilt. Years later, she discovered that Emma Grambly had hoped Harold would marry her daughter, Penelope.

Suddenly, standing before her sink, Lucy understands her pointed references to Calypso. Jacqueline's egg, resting on the towel beside the sink, positively glows.

•   ◆   •

Sunday, Mar. 11, 1888 Warm No eggs
First robin. Harold is nervous.

At the door of the church, Harold's father and mother.

"Never thought I'd see you married," his father said to Harold, and offered his hand in genuine congratulations.

His mother choked on her teeth.

"You're getting a fine girl," his father said as he shook Lucy's hand. He tried to make his eyes twinkle. All he could muster was a twitch.

Someone, off and to the left, muttered under his breath, "But he's getting the better in-laws." Lucy wanted to turn, quickly, to see who it was, to cut him with a look, but thought it might be better to pretend such comments were never uttered. Best to pretend they were never thought. It was harder to pretend that she didn't hear another comment, sotto voce, about chaperones and courtships. It was even harder to pretend that she hadn't recognized whose voice it was—Sally Mumsford. Lucy inhaled as much as her corset would allow, and exhaled slowly. Soon they would be away. Soon they would be home.

Chastity stood, patiently, in her harness. Harold took the reins and urged her quickly to a trot, a trot they held until they had cleared the town and crossed the creek. Then he brought her down to a walk, and she ambled along, her gray hairs beginning to show in her blonde coat, gray hairs Lucy hadn't noticed before. The mare was as old as herself, Lucy recalled. She couldn't remember a time before the two Belgians. Harold was excited. His cheeks were flushed, from the warm church and the sudden chill. Clouds had been moving in all morning. Thick, gray clouds. Harold began talking about getting a heavy-hunter.

"Jim Brandais has a good half-draft stud," he said. "Bergoyne out of Clovis. He's been throwing some nice foals."

Lucy caught herself holding her breath. She'd heard the same talk at Hutcheson's Feed. Jim Crandall and Boxer Reid and Fred McGinnis had been mulling over Jim Brandais's breeding for nearly a year.

"He's killing those mares," Fred McGinnis said one day while she was there. "Breeding Bergoyne to Thoroughbreds."

"But he's been throwing some nice foals," said Boxer. "As happy doing the heavy work as the light."

"Even temperament, too," said Jim Crandall. "Saw a storm flare up last September, and one of his yearlings didn't flinch. Had the rest of the herd prancing and blowing out."

"A good all-purpose horse," said Harold. "Good for the plow, good for riding out."

Chastity plodded along ahead of them. Lucy tried to smile. Their plow and harnesses were for a team of drafts, too heavy for a half-draft let alone a quarter-draft.

"Where do you want to go riding out?" Lucy asked.

"Oh, all over," said Harold. He held the reins lightly in his hands. Chastity knew the way home. The road was muddy and rutted; it was too early for that. Lucy heard a rumble.

"Was that thunder?"

Harold looked to the sky.

"Hope not," he said. "We sure don't need the rain."

They didn't get rain.

By the time Chastity turned in from the road, the snow was swirling. By the time they had unharnessed her and turned her out, put the wagon away, saw to Temperance and the chickens, four inches had fallen. By evening feed, it was a foot. By morning, two feet. By Wednesday, when the clouds finally lifted, four feet of thickly layered snow had fallen.

•　　•　　•

For four days Harold paced the house. He made forays with the shovel to clear paths to the barn and other outbuildings, and spent an hour here and there pacing the barn, the soft breathing of the horses underscoring his itch, his need to be doing something. Twice he was ready to hitch the team and work the driveway, but Lucy argued against it. Harold thought they might benefit from the work. He knew he would. Lucy was more patient. The storm would pass.

It hadn't taken him long to bring his possessions in from the barn. They left them on the wagon that first evening, in their excitement to complete the chores and get inside. The snow was offered as an excuse. By the end of the second day, however, Harold had tramped a narrow path between the barn and the house, while Lucy directed him through the kitchen and up to her parents' bedroom. It was difficult for her to think of it otherwise. She had continued in her own room after their deaths. Their room was larger and commanded a full view of the yard, the barn, and the fields that ran to the creek. Harold and Lucy moved into it in that first night of the swirling blizzard. The move had an odd effect on Lucy. For her entire life, her perspective from the house had been of the road and the field across the way—the same as the view from the kitchen. She never realized how odd the layout of the house was, with the kitchen in the "front," until many years later. The parlor and her parents' bedroom were away from the road. The movement from the front to the back came with an entirely different set of sounds. She could hear the horses and the chickens, even through the storm, from that back room. They were comforting, but she found herself attending to their subtle changes. She no longer heard the sweep and whoosh of the trees in the front when the wind came up. The back was decidedly quieter. Odder was the eastern window that brought the light in so early. Rather than waking her up, it sent her deeper into sleep, deeper under her pillow, and she found herself rising later, but more and more tired, as though the room itself wore her out. She didn't think that her growing tiredness had much to do with Harold, even as she was slowly conforming to his habits, staying up just a little later each night because he did, taking those few extra moments to walk through the house, closing curtains against the night chills and locking doors.

Harold didn't much like the room. It wasn't important to him, he simply didn't like the furniture. They'd moved it out in those stormy days, shifting chests of drawers, small stands, tables, and chairs from one room to the next, up the stairs, back down the stairs, moving the bed under the window, then back to the inside wall, all without resolution. He finally grew tired of thinking about it, as did Lucy, and they had left everything where it was when their interest waned, an interest that was nearly exhausted by the time the storm had spent itself. With the end of the storm, they were able to turn their attention outside again. It was several months before a chest of drawers in Lucy's old room was shoved against the wall, having been left in the middle of the floor.

Lucy quickly discovered that outdoors was their element. She enjoyed harnessing Chastity and Temperance and working the plow as much as Harold enjoyed breathing the air. She enjoyed working with him in the barn, taking inventory of the seed, readying the seeder for the field, for the melt. The melt itself came quickly enough. By early April, there were only pockets of snow. The path to the barn, hard-packed with their constant transit, held its own against the growing warmth and the sun. The ground itself, however, remained wet. The extra snow at the end of the season served mainly to insulate the frozen ground, and so it wasn't until the tenth of May that they were able to turn the soil. Chastity and Temperance led as they labored, Lucy wheeling bags of seed out to the team while Harold kept the rows straight. Once they got to it, the work went quickly enough. It was the waiting that was unbearable. Once the seeds were in, the summer offered more chores than two people could imagine. They often labored after dark, enjoying the smell of dirt and sweat and each other.

Lucy was happy.

Harold loved eggs. Each morning, he ate a full half-dozen— either scrambled or folded over.

He could taste the difference, he said, between the Araucanas' and the Hamburgs' and preferred the Hamburgs' eggs above all. Lucy pursed her lips when she learned this, but she didn't say anything. Her father had said the same. She herself ate two eggs, sometimes scrambled or folded, sometimes poached in honor of her mother, who claimed poaching was the only true way of preparing eggs, blue-shelled or other. Lucy hadn't poached them as much as she'd liked because it made her too sad to think of her mother. She hadn't wanted to be sad. She'd wanted more than anything to feel the unbridled excitement of racing Ethel to the creek, the thrill she had when she'd open the door to the coop each morning, strew corn, check the water, and then, only then, turn to the nest boxes to see how many blue jewels her chickens had made for her.

She still felt some of the excitement each morning as she removed her egg basket from the hook next to the kitchen door and stepped out into the world, but it was different. Perhaps, she thought, she missed her roosters, Victoria and Winifred, and their puffery. Perhaps she missed Maude. Maude had a way of forgetting that she was a hen. Every so often, she would chase Victoria and Winifred around the pen to claim the world for herself. It was hard for Lucy not to smile at the memory as she made her way across the yard to the coop.

Each night during the blizzard, she thought she could hear, under the sounds of snow blowing against the house, her chickens clucking and muttering. She lay awake, long past midnight, long past Harold's breathing became regular and calm, and listened to her birds. Martha Wayles fussed through the night. Lucretia and Dolley fought over a nest box well after two in the morning.

Each morning, during the blizzard, she woke to eggs and more eggs. She collected so many, and carried so many through the snow, that it nearly seemed as though each of her hens were laying two a day. Impossible, she thought, as she stroked their head feathers. The red and gold glowed against the gray and white skies. The feathers themselves were as finely articulated as the whirling snowflakes. She stroked their head feathers. Impossible.

•　　•　　•

Friday, Aug. 17, 1888 Hot 4 eggs
Eating breaks a sweat.

Lucy stood on the front porch, watching Harold recede. He turned just before he was lost to the horizon, and waved. It was all she could do to hold back her tears. Across the road, the hay, cut and laid out in evenly spaced rows, gave up its moisture to the heat; she could see the waves rising through the air. She thought about Ethel. She thought about Ethel's tears. She thought about her childhood. She felt the overwhelming sadness rise with the heat waves, and half sat, half collapsed into the swing. Her hands worked the strings of her apron, to free her growing stomach of the extra layer of cotton.

Harold had been acting strangely. Since the solstice, since the solstice egg, round and double yolked (double the sunshine, she'd joked), she'd had caught him looking over his shoulder as though he were chased by demons. In the field, behind the team, he couldn't seem to hurry them enough. In the barn, he'd kept his face to the aisle as he mucked the stalls. He'd watched the road, looking at it ten to twenty times a day, as if waiting for news. She'd caught him gazing out the window at night.

"What if," he'd said, suddenly, as if breaking out of a trance, "what if you need help when it's time? What if I can't get help quick enough?"

The question had offered its own kind of relief. Suddenly, she had been able to read his eyes again, and read their worry, their concern.

All he could talk about was a telephone. A telephone, he'd said, would save half the time if she needed help. Instead of him racing to town to get the doctor, they could call. He'd had it all worked out: the fastest he could get to town was to halter one of the drafts, leap on it bareback, and urge it to take the five miles at a trot. He'd figured Chastity could cover the distance in forty minutes, plus haltering and rousting the doctor—an hour all told. That, assuming the doctor was home. It would be another hour and a half by the time the doctor harnessed his own team, hitched the wagon, and traveled the same five miles to the farmhouse. Two and a half hours, he'd said, sketching the numbers in the dirt, and that's in daylight. His eyes had met hers. And that's if the weather is fine. Snow, hail, a blizzard?!

"Imagine the worst!" he'd said. "Imagine the worst."

She had. She'd imagined the worst would be the threat to her unborn in those two and one-half hours, and to be alone and unable to do anything about it.

And just as suddenly, she realized that she *would* be alone and would be unable to do anything about it.

She lost him to the horizon, just as he had emerged from it—only a year before. It seemed longer, like a lifetime had passed in those twelve months. And now he was gone. He would talk to the telephone man, just as he'd said he would. He would talk to him about installing the wires, and the costs of the poles, and who they might find to dig the holes, and whether or not the telephone man would pay for all of it, or whether they would have to bring something to the table to trade, a cow, two cows, half the hay in the field, anything.

He would talk to the telephone man, just as he'd said he would. He would strike a deal. And then, satisfied that he had taken care of her better than if he were there by her side, he would continue over the horizon.

Lucy sat, quiet, on the front porch, the hay in the field across the road giving up its moisture as she held back hers. She couldn't imagine where he would go, what he would do. Would he go north? South? East? West? Each was equally absurd. He wasn't interested in the city. Nor did it seem to her that he would enjoy ten minutes on a ship. Clerking was too confining. Mining, prospecting—too risky. Harold liked the sure thing. Harold had a heart of gold. She fingered the apron strings, wrapping one around and around itself in a semblance of a knot. She imagined him racing across the field, his hair flying, his mouth open to catch the wind, racing toward her, and shook off a premonition of his death. The apron fell to the porch as she stood, already forgotten.

The hay would still need to be brought in, Harold or no, baby or no.

She completed her chores. The line of her jaw remained rigid throughout the feeding, watering, and haying of the horses, and the feeding and bedding down of the chickens. Mary Todd fussed and walked the rail; Jaunty Girl, just three months old, peeped and peeped and peeped. She worked through the garden, patiently, picking just enough lettuce and peas for herself, culling the wilted leaves for the chickens and an occasional pea as a treat. Then she moved to the rows of strawberries and collected a handful, and then another quart or more for the Westers. She hard-boiled an egg, Lucretia's from the feel of the shell, chopped it up, and sprinkled it over the bed of greens and raw peas. She and Ethel had eaten so many peas that they had to lay themselves out in the yard, moaning with their distended bellies. They tortured each other by rolling over and pushing on the stretched skin, feeling for evidence of the little round vegetables. There was plenty of evidence. Lucy remembered that she could feel the lumps in Ethel's stomach, so many inexplicable lumps! How could it be? They'd chewed and chewed the sweet green peas, chewed them into a mash, and still they lumped in their bellies! Ethel cried out so loudly at Lucy's touch that Lucy grew frightened and was about to run for help when her own stomach cramped and set her rolling about on her back and slapping the grass with her open hands as she spasmed "ow ow ow ow ow" in the growing dusk. That set Ethel to the giggles, and they alternately cried with the pain and laughed with the silliness of their pea bellies. They lay there until well after dark, until the cramping stopped and they were able to make their way to the house.

Lucy still had an hour of sun by the time she finished her salad. Her jaw softened with her thoughts of Ethel. She washed the strawberries, ate the small handful that she had picked for herself, and put the rest in a bowl. Then she set out for the Westers, her footsteps following the path that Harold had taken a few hours earlier. There was no trace of his transit. Walking felt good, even in the humidity. The swinging of her hips loosened her back. She paused in the low spots where the coolness rose from the hollows, paused until the deerflies drove her along. The sun sat full and round on the horizon by the time she arrived with her strawberry offering.

It had dipped below the horizon by the time she started home, firing the undersides of clouds with a soft red-purple. The deerflies were replaced by June bugs, stupidly knocking about, and an occasional mosquito. Warren and Ernestine were amenable. Their teenage son, Melvin, would help her with the hay and with any other chores she might find too much for her. They laughed with her about Harold's dreams of the telephone. Their kitchen was comfortable, their laughter was warm and welcoming, and it took Lucy an enormous effort step out into the dusk. But the world, too, was alive and laughing as she walked. She would manage. She would manage just fine, she thought. She felt her heart lighten, and she tried her feet, setting them to skip and skip and skip. The humidity was dissolving even as the fog began rising from the creek.

•   •   •

Dec. 21 Ice 1 egg
Helen.

There was no telephone. Nor was it needed. No one had imagined the worst, the most horrific, that which needed no doctor, that which needed no telephone. Ernestine came by around noon to check on her and to throw a few bales of hay down for the horses. Melvin could have worked the hay later, but Ernestine just wanted to be sure it was done. They had a cup of tea. Ernestine, concerned. Lucy, tired. Lucy promised again to signal any need she might have and pointed to the red cloth and the candle, at the ready.

Lucy tended to the horses as darkness fell. The shortened day left her little time to complete all that needed to be done, and she saved her chickens for last. The horses were happy enough working their hay. She broke the ice in their trough. She walked through the paddock to secure the gate to the pasture. She opened a new bag of feed and emptied it in the bin. She had to use an old scoop to shovel the grain into the bin and it took that much longer before she was done with the horses.

Her chickens were already on their roosts when she entered the coop. They watched her, indifferently at first, and then with a bit more interest. Then, one by one, Martha Wayles, Lucretia, Dolley, Mary Todd, Martha D., Rachel, Anna Symmes, Lucy Ware, Eliza, Jaunty Girl, Beauty, Dame Maude, Lightning Bolt, Racer, Cimmaron, and Red jumped from the rail to the floor, a series of clucking squawks amidst a flurry of beating wings. They circled her, heads cocked, eyeing her, strutting and preening counterclockwise. Lucy felt an oddness to their behavior and strew cracked corn about the floor. More odd was that they ignored the corn and kept their focus on her. She began backing out of the coop, when suddenly her first contraction dropped her to her knees. The chickens moved closer as she gasped for air; Anna Symmes suddenly leapt to her shoulder and stepped onto her head. Lucy felt the hen's feet, talons, strong and sharp against her skin, her hair beginning to tangle with the hen's movements. She screamed. The chickens retreated, all except for Anna Symmes, who flapped her wings in her own attempt to free her feet of Lucy's hair. But they didn't come free. Her wings beat down about her head, about her ears and face, and she screamed again, and again when the second contraction struck. She rolled out of the coop and kicked shut the door. Temperance snorted. Chastity stood stock still, holding her breath. Lucy felt an hour slip past before her heart slowed. Chastity finally exhaled and resumed her steady grinding of hay. Lucy braced herself against the wall as the next contraction came, and then another.

It was seven-thirty by the time Lucy regained the house. She was cold. She was tired. She was hungry. She lit the candle and put it in the window, and sat by the fire, dozing. Contracting. Dozing. Ernestine and Melvin arrived around ten. Ernestine immediately set about making something to eat and heating water. Melvin, after seeing that his mother had everything she needed, left for town. Lucy dreamt of Ethel that night, dreamt of her running free through the pasture, pretending to be chickens, swimming in the creek, laughing, happy, and warm.

The doctor arrived in the morning. By late afternoon, Lucy had given birth to her daughter, Helen. Stillborn.

•   •   •

Lucy wrinkles her nose. A gust of wind has filled her with the smell of rot, and an immeasurable recall—she was six again, and standing on a stone wall looking down. The stones were sharp and jutting, and a dank odor rose from the rich and rotting leaves turning to loam and playing home to a thousand creeping bugs and snakes. She hadn't meant to be scared, hadn't meant to be afraid of the wall, or the distance to the ground—the grass wasn't as comforting as she remembered. Her feet felt the stones as she edged along. She had forgotten why she was on the wall, whether it came of a deep urge to conquer her own fears, or because she was following Ethel, when a false step set a stone, vividly mottled, vividly black on white, like a dream, in motion; it wobbled, her ankle twisted, and the pain. . . . Again the ground, the rot and dankness, and the sudden appearance of her father's feet, and then, her father's arms ready to catch her.

She felt herself collapse, a capitulation rather than a saving gesture, and fell into his arms. With that rescue came a new calamity, the odor of the wall, of the loam, the rotting leaves; that odor was her father, and she pushed away, pushed away to be free of it. He set her safely on the ground, and she hobbled home by his side, her hand tenuously in his. But she has never been free of the odor; it hangs on her every remembrance of him. It hangs in the kitchen, the smell of rotting leaves, the smell of the cemetery, the smell of Friday, the smell of vertigo, the smell of Harold walking away, twisting to wave his final good-bye.

That spring, she heard the rumors. Each Friday she would go to town, each Friday they had saved the latest for her: had she heard from Harold? Rumors (sotto voce but loud enough for her to hear) had him dying of tetanus in the Florida swamps, marrying a Southern Belle, dying of typhoid in Maryland, building trestles on the Mississippi, killing hogs in Chicago, marrying a Wisconsin Dairy Queen, until finally and unequivocally dying of shame while pandering in the panned-out gold bust of California or Mexico or Chile or Spain. Perhaps a generous and sympathetic inclination to one's neighbors led these voices to further characterize him as unshaven and unbathed, a sloven laggard whose steady physical decline was precipitated by his moral trespass. She cursed her spring chickens with names of places they'd never see: Augustine, Friendly, Natchez, and Bernardino.

She laid Helen to rest in the smudge of winter. She laid Helen to rest beside Ethel.

3

Owing to the recent crisis, the Mayor of Homer has concluded that ragweed is out of control. He asks that all persons not suffering the effects of the pernicious weed to eradicate it by any and all means possible.

—Homer *Ode*, July 10th, 1896

Lucy wrinkles her nose. Her eyes crinkle, pinch half shut with the trace of rot. The flowers, the trees, the yard blur and she sees the smudges on the window—sees the glass itself with its sworls and imperfections. She sees a shadowy half reflection of her hands washing an egg, its shell pitted and ridged with its own imperfections.

It was Friday. She could not remember when she'd begun looking in the mirror. She could not remember when she'd begun brushing her hair as part of her day, as something that needed to be done as surely as feeding her chickens. She could not remember when she'd begun to consider her hair as having a color—or what color it had been. She could remember a "coming to," but to what? She'd been seated in her room, in the morning, her hands had played with her hair in the mirror—she'd become conscious of the mirror before her, conscious of its frame—a dark wood of unknown origin with golden leaves painted on it . . . conscious of the silver behind the glass . . . conscious of the glass itself, and all in desperate need of a cleaning. These were, however, digressions, avoidances, deferrals, for what she had become truly conscious of—

She had become someone else.

She had lost something, and in that loss, there was a new being.

She cast her eyes about the room, looking for the difference, searching for the change. The room, however, was the same as it had always been. Nor did it strike her that this new self was seeing it with "new" eyes. The room was the same as it had always been, the same as it was before she was born. The bed was covered with her grandmother's crazy quilt as it had been since her grandmother was a girl. The stand, carved from branches of a hickory, hadn't been moved in decades. On it were a shell her grandfather had given her grandmother when they were courting and a small, bluish rock she'd found in the creek when playing with Ethel years before. The curtains moved, but only with the breeze. She noted that they could stand a cleaning. The window framed the massive and ancient oaks, just as it always had. The trees might have grown, imperceptibly, in the last twenty years.

The mirror, too, was the same. It had been her mother's. "A contribution to her vanity," Maureen Kesling had said to Emma Grambly in those early years before Lucy's father began going to Rome. Maureen Kesling's face was pinched, but not so tight as to prevent her tongue from wagging, and Emma doted on her, doted on her reports of what everyone and anyone purchased in a given day. Lucy'd sat in her mother's lap as her mother combed her hair, two faces reflecting in the glass, two faces laughing with the static in her hair, static that crackled with each stroke and sent strand after strand skyward.

But the face in the glass showed a change. She studied it, studied her hair and its slow evolution from brown to gray, and her forehead, which seemed more pronounced than it had as a child. Her eyes were penetrating. They stared into her as she stared into them. They were brown, brown as they always had been, but there seemed to be so many more tiny bits of green than there had been the last time she really looked at herself. Her nose was strong, in three-quarter view. Her lips were set. But her eyes bore into her, and bore the flecks of imperfection like the mirror, like the glass.

She turned to give herself to a full view of her face, and as she turned, she caught something, something imperceptible, inexplicable. She brought her hand up, slowly. Her fingers touched her face, as though she was getting to know herself, as though she'd never known the woman in the glass. With that touch she suddenly recognized in her countenance what had not been there before: a smile, a smile buried in the pursing of her lips, in the curves around her mouth, but a smile that hung about her mouth, about her face as invisible as the summer air.

It baffled her for a moment; but her bafflement turned to marvel—the shades of feelings, the flickering of her growing recognition, *made no impression in the glass.* Not the tiniest turn in the corners of her mouth. Not the smallest crease around her nose. Not the slightest wrinkle about her eyes. She nearly burst out loud laughing at the sight, and in return, could barely detect the faintest of twinkles in her eyes, the faintest shimmering of green against the brown. No, the faintest twinkle was always there, as if she were always about to laugh out loud! Her hand rose to her mouth with the surprise. Surely the mirror worked, for it caught her hand as it rose, caught the surprise itself. But it failed completely to register the smile that she felt bursting across her face!

She didn't know when it happened. Surely she had been a child when she cavorted with Ethel, dancing about the land. Laughing. Smiling. Surely she had been a child when Harold came to call.

The clock chimed the hour and she quickly finished coiling her hair and setting her crown with pins before leaving the mirror and its revelations.

Outside, the dew was still on the ground—her footprints to the barn and the coop from early in the morning were visible, as were Cinder's tracks, crisscrossing the yard, a maniacal display of doggish exuberance. The tracks were vivid, vibrant, and she wondered, briefly, if they would show up in her mirror, or, if they did, if their intensity would be reflected. She surveyed the grounds, the barn, the coop, the grass leading down to the creek. All of it had a clarity, a brilliance this morning. She made a number of mental notes: the three stones that had come loose in the foundation of the barn would need to be reset, two small trees that grew against the coop would have to go, and the harnesses needed a thorough cleaning. The dirt nearly leapt from them, she thought, as she harnessed the team. Yellow and Gold stood patiently as she hitched the wagon. They were Chastity's foals, coming on four years, and steady, despite their age. Cinder barked. Excited. Ready to be off.

Lucy added the two racks of eggs to the two fishermen's creels she'd just completed. Two racks of eggs that she'd collected all week. Had anyone been there to ask, she could have identified for each egg the hen that laid it. It was a growing flock. Two years before, she had added to her chicken coop, knocking out one wall in the process, and adding a seemingly endless array of nest boxes. There were forty hens all told. She knew them all. Knew each egg.

She urged the horses forward, to the road and to the right, where the town of Homer awaited. It was Friday.

Even at a walk, the wagon listed to the left and right from the ruts and pockets. She knew the eggs would suffer for it, but she had become accustomed to the shaking and the foreknowledge. Cinder raced off to the south, drawn by frantic display of ducks rising in the dawn, by the rustling of turkeys as they began their day, by the echo of the creaking wagon off a rock face. Drawn by anything. Everything.

She had never thought of leaving.

Not after Helen. Not after Harold. Not even during the crisis of '93. Never.

Warren was haying as she passed, and he paused to wave. Lucy called out a hello and Cinder dashed off to greet him. Lucy urged the horses on without stopping; if the Westers wanted her to pick up something in town, they would have tied a cloth to the post at the road. Warren returned to his haying and disappeared behind a stand of birches. Moments later, Cinder emerged from the gray-white trunks and trotted along with the horses for the next mile or more, past the Moultons' place. She stood in the creek, soaking her feet and lapping at the water. She trotted ahead, and within a mile, Lucy could hear her startled barking. The wagon lurched from side to side, until Lucy could see that Cinder had encountered a road crew. She whistled, and the dog hurried back, hackles raised, and leapt into the back of the wagon. Four men were busy filling in the ruts, filling in the pockets made from horses' hooves, working the road with their shovels and rakes and tampions. They nodded at Lucy as she passed. As the horses moved onto the newly reworked ground, the wagon immediately ceased its swaying. It was too late for the eggs, of course, but no one in Homer would notice. Lucy appreciated the roadwork for the better footing it provided her horses, but she knew there was little concern for horses in the raking, shoveling, and filling in of ruts and holes. The road crew was working out from the main streets of Homer for the automobiles. So said the *Ode*, at least. The town council had approved the extra work. One of the council members thought they might best ban horses from the town. The future, he said, lay in the automobile. The future, he said, did not include horse manure on the streets of Homer.

The Lamarques' horses pranced in their pasture as they caught sight of Yellow and Gold. Cinder leapt from the wagon to protect them, trotting between the wagon and the pasture line, while the Thoroughbreds snorted and blew out. They topped the ridge and Homer came into view, the church steeple first, then the third floor of the Homer Hotel.

Something about her newfound knowledge turned her into the cemetery as she entered the town, rather than at the end of her Friday as had become her normal habit. She wanted to tell Ethel, to share with her this secret laughter she'd discovered. She followed the path around to the back, but immediately recognized her mistake. Emma Grambly had passed. Her funeral meant Lucy did not have the cemetery to herself. Cinder rode, quietly, in the wagon beside her. The horses paused at the sight of another wagon and the handful of people who had gathered around to wish the gossip well in her future. The diggers had trampled the grass around Emma's new grave, and around those in the surrounding neighborhood, including her great great grandfather, cofounder of all that was glorious in the town of Homer. The grass was stomped flat, and dirt lay everywhere, as though the diggers had amused themselves by flinging it in all directions by the shov-elful. All Lucy could think was how Emma would not approve. Nor would she approve of the small turnout—no more than a dozen of the town's finest had broken away from the routines of their days to pay their respects. Nor would she approve of the new monu-ment to Haskins. Haskins's kin had pooled their money in tribute of their founding father and had built a mausoleum. The Hey-woods and Gramblys had grumbled, but no one had mentioned it to Emma in her confinement. It overshadowed the Heywoods in the early morning. In the evening, the Gramblys were eclipsed.

The minister prattled. Lucy turned the horses down a different path and felt the smile creeping about her face. It tugged at the corners of her mouth, pulling and stretching itself all the way around to behind her ears. It grew bigger, nearly bursting with Lucy's knowledge that it was invisible to the world. On the bench beside her, Cinder broke into a smile of her own, punctuated by her panting. The horses moved on, around to the back, out of sight of the entrance, but, unfortunately, not out of sight of the dozen mourners, whose eyes remained fixed on the minister, or on the casket, or on the mound of dirt. Ashes to ashes, dirt to dirt. Lucy smiled and stepped down from the wagon.

The minister prattled on. Lucy could hear the sound of him from the low ground near Ethel's and Helen's stones. His words, however, were swallowed by the death that surrounded them. Cinder jumped from the wagon and pressed her nose into Lucy's hand. Lucy turned her back on the Protestant ceremony and sur-veyed the stones, old stones, that graced the area. The weeds grew up around them, gloriously, she thought, and she stepped through the grasses. A soft rustle broke through the prattling, a snake slipping off a bit of exposed rock as she approached. She paused at Ethel's stone and beheld the women around her—Marie and Nelly and Jacqueline and Mary Ellen and Sarah and Hannah and Abigail—beheld them with a deeper appreciation for what they had done, what Ethel had done. They had left. They had abandoned the world. She felt it, the abandonment, felt the depth of its hurt. It ached. Lucy continued to smile, perhaps from the pain, perhaps to cover it, perhaps a hundred things, but she continued to smile as she knelt by Ethel's grave. The minister had stopped. Or if he still prattled on, the wind had risen to whisk his words away. But if the wind had risen, it had neglected to ruffle the trees, for everything stilled as Lucy grinned underneath.

She began plucking weeds, on the verge of saying something. She thought back to the farm, to Ethel's hair and the way it flew and the sound of her laughter. She felt the muscles in her face relax, felt the breeze catch a stray wisp of her hair and dance it across her forehead. She pulled at the weeds carefully and thought back to their futures, to the promises of the World Fair. She felt the words forming in her chest. She heard Ethel laugh. Around her, everything was stilled, focused on her hands and their slowed movement as they grasped and pulled. She felt the words rising, ready to burst through her own smile.

Beside her, Cinder issued the lowest of growls, barely audible over the silence.

Lucy turned quickly, away from Ethel, away from Helen, away from the women around her, toward the people who clustered about Emma Grambly's grave. A small child, maybe three years old, perhaps a girl, had strayed from the funeral and wandered over the dead toward Lucy. She wobbled from foot to foot, her head tucked up in a cap with a string drawn tight around her throat. She was engulfed in a light blue coat, oversized, that draped to her knees. Her fingers poked out from the ends of the sleeves. Her knees were covered with dirt. Cinder relaxed and lay down at Lucy's side.

The small girl wobbled closer, babbling something that was stolen by the breeze. She was looking at Lucy, looking at Cinder, as she came on. Her left hand stretched out to the side to touch a stone (Lucy knew it was Alphonse and Mimi Gros's stone, a polished marble memorial to Homer's apple orchard owners). The girl stretched her hand to the stone, but her fingers merely brushed it. She seemed for a moment about to fall, but she regained her balance with her next step. Her mouth continued to move, issuing a stream of sounds that were inaudible to Lucy.

Lucy sat back on her haunches, watching the girl come nearer and nearer. Helen would have been six by now. Would have been starting her own flock of chickens. Would have commanded all that she could see from her bedroom window, Lucy's old bedroom. Would have run for the sheer joy of running. Kindred spirit of Cinder.

The child came on, trying to free herself of her clothes. She came on, tromping over the Gros graves, over the Stubens, over the Lambs. The breeze swirled, brushed Lucy in the face, brought her a single word—puppy.

Suddenly, a scream. It broke through the relative stillness. It washed over the grass and the stones. Cinder growled again, a low growl. Her hackles rose. The girl accelerated. Her face was set, focused straight ahead, but it pinched and reddened with the knowledge that her mother was running to catch her. It burst into tears with the foreknowledge that her mother *would* catch her before she reached the dog.

Lucy could not hear the girl's tears. She remained on her haunches and watched Penelope Grambly fly across the grass. Penelope gained on her daughter, her arms flailing, her hair loosed from under her bonnet, her skirts rising and falling; her eyes wide with fear, she was out of control, racing maniacally toward her daughter. The girl tried to move faster, but could not within the confines of her clothing.

Behind her, the small group of mourners paused. Their eyebrows came together with the stern understanding of what was happening. Only the minister's mouth was open and it remained so, somewhere in the middle of a blessing, a blessing disrupted by the dead woman's granddaughter.

Penelope's scream continued to reverberate through the cemetery. The cedars could not absorb its shrill piercing. Penelope gained her daughter, and with a swoop she snatched the girl's arm and brought her to an abrupt halt. It nearly yanked the girl's arm right off her body. The suddenness of it silenced the daughter. The success of it silenced the mother. For a moment, the cemetery was quiet again.

The wind swirled.

The daughter burst into fresh tears.

Penelope burst with punctured breath, "Stay . . . Away . . . From . . . There!"

They turned. The girl tried to look back, but the coat, or the cap, or the pulling on her arm made it impossible.

Lucy collapsed, sat on the ground next to Cinder, all thoughts of Ethel flung from her head. She had heard it before, had heard the tone, had heard the "Stay away from *her*," had heard the taunts of the young boys with their oddly skewed insults sung as they rode their bicycles alongside her wagon, "Egg Lady, Egg Lady is an Old Maid, Egg Lady Egg Lady gives Eggs in Trade." She had heard it before, but she had never understood. Oh, Lucy understood Penelope's damnation as she sat, watching the woman recede. She recognized it with all the clarity with which she had seen her own smile.

Her hand drifted out and landed on Cinder's head. She idly scratched the dog behind her ears and along her back.

Her hand drifts out to wipe a smudge from the window.

But Lucy didn't understand. She didn't understand Sally Mumsford. She didn't understand Ellen Mackinaw, with her white gloves and sidereal glances. She didn't understand Joanne Walker, who spoke of roses and weeds whenever Lucy drew near. She didn't understand the Ladies Auxiliary.

Her jaw set. The mourners retreated. Emma Grambly's body was lowered into the hole. The diggers began throwing dirt.

Lucy turned, back to Ethel, back to Helen, back to the weeds—toadflax and thistle—that graced their stones. She decided she liked them and left Helen's grave vibrant and overgrown.

.　.　.

The town council has approved numerous improvements to the town and has contracted with Jasperson & Sons to effect them. Citizens should be advised that many of Irish nation will be working on these improvements. Everyone is asked to treat them well. . . .

—Homer *Ode*, August 4th, 1908

Lucy sat on a bench inside the gate to the cemetery. The bench was new, wrought iron and uncomfortable, a reminder to the living that this bench could not be a final resting point. The iron nearly cut into her back. But she hardly noticed it given the envelope in her hand. Nor did she notice the gate, more iron, and fence, more iron that the town had installed to contain the dead. A year before, maybe more, Leonard Turner had been buried on the edge of the grounds, and with little fanfare and less authority. It turned out that he had been buried on land owned by Abraham Whitting, not within the cemetery proper. The stink *that* had raised might have been smelled all the way to Rome. Hence the fence. Not to protect the dead from the living, but to protect the living from the dead.

Lucy hardly noticed anything, given the envelope in her hand. She had thought Harold might be dead. She had hoped he wasn't, but the lack of news had troubled her. Even during the farm crisis, one heard news. The Crandalls had made it northwest of Chicago. The Motts had taken a southern route and had settled in Oklahoma. But there had been nothing of Harold. Nothing in the idle conversations at Kesling's. Nothing in the feed store. Nothing.

Suddenly, here was an envelope in her hand, in his hand. Her hand shook as she turned it over and over—the lack of return address, the stamp canceled one, two, three times or more, the folds and creases, all of these mark how far away Harold was. How far away he had always been. How far away he had been back then, even as they'd moved furniture to accommodate him, even as he'd moved about the farmyard. She broke her gaze for a moment and took a deep breath. The iron bench pressed into her back, but she didn't feel it. The glue gave way quickly. The letter nearly fell out and into her hands. They shook with trepidation.

Dear Harold Jr.

I write now that you are a man and I write to you as a man to a man, and to tell you of your duty to the world. The world is a vast place, full of excitement and danger. No doubt the brothers who have soared in the air have caught your imagination. The recent tragedy in California has no doubt caught your sympathy. Consider always that you are a man among men, and have responsibilities. Consider always that what you do will bear unexpected fruits. As an example, I offer the Mayor of Cowen, who bowed to the sentiment that the town had fallen into hard times. He ordered all property owners to plant tulips so that they might be born again with the beautiful blossoms in the spring. The entire town burst itself with civic pride and planted more than 6,000 bulbs. Winter passed into Spring. The tender shoots began to emerge. But instead of a blooming town, there was blooming skunks—a thousand skunks come to eat the bulbs. The mayor tried to chase them away with his dogs, but the stench they released engulfed the town in a cloud so black that none of its citizens were ever seen again.

Remember always your mother is a fine woman.

Your Father

Lucy sat for a full half an hour without moving. She didn't know what to think about the letter, about Harold, about Helen. The story was for her. She knew it; why else would he write of such a silly thing? She had told him of the skunk in the chicken house, of Ethel's fears that night, so long ago that she had nearly forgotten it. She worried that she had forgotten so much. She caught the faintest smell of sweat.

She peered from underneath her hat at the stones around her. She had begun wearing hats. Not that she had many, but she wore them. Not that she hoped to be stylish, but she preferred the way they protected her from the sun, and from the rain, and from the knowing looks of the town as she passed. She was better able to ignore the greetings and snubbings alike.

A fresh mound of dirt gave off the promise of turned soil. A new stone had been planted, and at its base, flowers. Sally Mumsford had passed away. Lucy'd already forgotten how she'd died, though she'd read it in the *Ode.* It could have been tuberculosis or jungle fever or a migraine in her foot for all she could remember. As she peered out from under her hat, however, she did remember Sally as a younger woman, as a vain and shallow woman who'd sniffed at Chastity and called her a broken-down mare. Sally had been wearing a new riding coat and had been striking a pose outside of Macer's Print Shop. The pose had been for the town and for Alan Macer. The Macers had moved away with the farm crisis, leaving an empty building.

Lucy pauses in the rinsing of an egg and recalls that Macer's Print Shop is now the Rialto Theater, where they show movies. Just the Friday before, Lucy had been tempted to see Helene Chadwick starring in *Women Who Dare.* As she stands at her sink, she wishes she'd dared to cut Sally so many years before and doesn't think any worse of herself for thinking ill of the dead. She doesn't think any worse of herself for wondering if shallow people were buried in shallow graves, or if the pious were buried closer to God.

The iron cut into her back. Mostly, Sally had posed for Sally. She'd been worked up over her Morgan and her new bridle or saddle or some other bit of tack, and she'd seen Chastity standing in her harness, with Lucy clambering up into the wagon, and she'd struck a pose and pointed to the old mare with her crop and waggled it around. Now Sally was dead, worked by Effing, the embalmer, into a permanent pose. Her stone was new. The soil was freshly shoveled and raked and already crusting over.

Lucy sat, alone, in the cemetery, Harold's letter in hand, the recall coloring the world before her. It was just like Harold to presume a son. To presume himself multiplied. Lucy braced herself against the bench. Everything was cast in green, the grass, the leafing out of the trees, the sky, everything but the stones, white and stretching out in a semblance of order, lines curving out of kilter, lines aborted, lines clustered and isolated. Some stones had toppled and peeked through the long grass, vestigial reminders. She sat in the cemetery, Harold's letter in hand, and felt a flush run through her body. Through the green, she heard the faint baa-ing of sheep. She was vaguely aware of the nudge at her feet: one of the sheep had ventured close and was grazing there. She was vaguely aware of the rest of the flock as it moved across the grass, grazing the graves. It was Horace Wobrun's flock come to town twice a summer to graze the dead. They grazed, white against the green, two clumps of white, three, four; they moved slowly, teeth grinding in perfect unison, almost as if orchestrated, even as a bit of bark dropped from one of the old willows and scattered them in all directions, streaking lines of white until they settled themselves again amidst the stones, filling in the green. Lucy felt the flush in her feet, her legs, her stomach. The sheep continued to graze; they clustered around a bit of clover that claimed Emma Grambly. One or two wandered to the vetch that overran LeFleur. Small hoof-prints punctured the freshly turned soil that covered Sally Mumsford. A heron rose from the river and sent the three that had wandered close to the water into short-lived spasms—their fear was contagious; three, four, five more jumped with surprise, white puffs folding, contracting, fear spread outward, like a wave, and spent itself just as quickly amidst the stones. Lucy felt the flush in her hands, her arms, her shoulders. One broke from a stone in an odd frenzy, as though she'd eaten something that drove her momentarily out of her mind, and then just as quickly settled to eating again. Through it all, the steady sound of teeth against teeth. It was almost comforting, the random movements, white on green, white on gray-green as the sun faded and dusk came on.

Yellow nickered, bringing Lucy out of her trance. She rose and scratched the Belgian's ear and buried her nose in the smell of the mare.

•   •   •

Heywood's Home for Boys closed last Thursday. Citizens have been alerted to possible criminal activity. To date, only three acts of minor vandalism have been reported.
>   —Homer *Ode*, September 1st, 1912

Lucy paused on her walk through the cemetery, the sound of an approaching automobile filling the air. She caught glimpses of it through the cedars and elms and the iron fence that lined the edge of the cemetery. It was a black skeletal thing that flickered behind the trees. The roaring and squeaking, however, were incessant. As it neared, she could see that it was driven by Robin Haskins, who hid behind goggles and roared with his own pleasure at the sheer noise of it all. It was as though he had been loosed upon the world, straight from hell, and was celebrating his recent freedom.

The automobile barely turned the corner before she heard another, rasping and wheezing, another black skeleton jumping and jigging toward her. The driver was different, though hiding behind goggles and dressed somewhat the same, otherwise she might be tempted to think it was the same devilish vehicle racing around and around the cemetery, the same devil condemned to screaming itself in circles around the dead.

She wondered, briefly, idly, whether the noise would have any effect on her eggs. It didn't really matter, because her eggs were safely out of her care, delivered to Kesling an hour before. Next door, a small crowd had assembled outside of Woolworths. There were bolts of cotton mixed with manikins wearing large-brimmed hats to protect them from the sun as they sipped from inexpensive tea sets.

None of the window dressings had held their interest, however. Nor was there anything for their eyes; it was their ears that had been caught: Woolworths had begun piping music into the street by affixing speakers to the outside of the building under the awning. A march had filled the air. Effing and Turner and Cob had tapped their feet to the sound. A couple of boys had begun their own parade. They'd saluted, with a rigid imprecision. They'd marched in step, in perfect control for ten or fifteen steps, before breaking into a rousing game of tag. They'd broken their formation, like a burst of pheasants flying up in all directions, wings in a flurry. Effing and Turner and Cob had tapped their feet in time with the music.

It had scraped at Lucy's ears, like nails on tin. The world had become noisy.

• • •

Lucy paused on her walk through the cemetery. In the twenty-two years that Woolworths had been in Homer, Lucy had never been inside. Her father had spurned Kesling's because Kesling had used a cash register and refused to record the transactions with paper and pen. Lucy had no such worries and had been trading eggs with Josh Kesling for years. In 1889, when the hammering began in the building next to Kesling's, Josh had remarked that all Woolworths were the same. Woolworth had opened his first five and dime up in Utica in 1879. Since then, he had opened stores in Syracuse, Rome, Albany, Ithaca, and a host of other towns in the middle of the state.

"And each one is identical to all the rest," Josh had said when the hammering began. "You want a basket? You find the same selection of baskets in every Woolworths." He'd pointed at Lucy's egg basket, the one her mother had made from willow so many years ago. Lucy still worked in willow, cutting and dragging branches over the ground, sweeping clean everything in their path while the willow witches protested every step. She also worked in ash, mostly ash for the creels she made for the fishermen.

"You won't find anything like that," Josh had said. "No. Frank Woolworth's got a plan."

Lucy had stood in the middle of Kesling's in the chaos that surrounded her. Jars of pickles were next to Lucy's baskets and creels. Fishing flies were surrounded by a book on baking, a small wrench, and sewing needles. There were dolls next to apples next to inkwells. Clearly, Josh Kesling didn't have a plan.

Sunderson had been unhappier still. He had mounted a campaign against Frank Woolworth and had taken it to the mayor's office, to little effect.

"It will be the death of my business," he'd said.

It had been.

Sunderson's Confectionery had gone bankrupt within two years. A year later, the farm crisis had struck, and Sunderson had blamed that on Woolworths as well. Lucy never figured that. But she had mourned the loss of the confectionery and the smell of chocolate that filled the street. So much better than the tin music and the exhaust from the automobiles. She could hear George Heywood responding—What about the manure? With a pointed look at her team.

The cemetery organization had tried to ban her team from the cemetery—citing the manure. They'd settled for a compromise. She could park her wagon just inside the gates where they'd made a special place for her and sunk a hitching post to make sure she didn't stray.

The emptiness deep inside rose again, as it had, off and on.

She took in a breath, took in the surroundings. There were so many more stones than there had been years ago, all those years ago. The emptiness rose as she moved closer and closer to Helen's grave. There was so much she had wanted to share.

Sunderson's grave lay nearby. It surprised her, surprised her for being so close to the "old maids," but surprised her more for the egg that was engraved in the stone. A flood of memories overcame her, nearly drowning her. Sunderson had had the most exquisite windows in town: she and Ethel had spent hours looking at the chocolate village of Homer that he'd created; there had been chocolate horses and chocolate dogs. Chocolate pigs and rabbits. Sunderson had even put a chocolate cat on the roof of Heinson's Grain and Feed. It had been curled up, as if in sleep. He had replicated the four cemeteries that graced the town. Though the girls had never noticed in all their hours with their faces pressed against the glass, Sunderson had recreated each stone, each stone as it went in, and with it, the inscription. Even the Anfalls' noses had been delicately carved in white chocolate. Sunderson had been the true town historian.

Lucy missed Sunderson's Confectionery, with the replica of Homer and the chocolate eggs. Ethel had loved the mint fillings and the sweetened raspberry fillings, and anything that was strange or exotic. Lucy had preferred the melted white custard that surrounded a yellow yolk of sugared lemon.

Lucy missed Ethel.

In that awful year, she'd seen her parents' stones recreated in Sunderson's window. Later, Ethel's stone had appeared. She'd almost felt she could visit their graves by standing on the street outside Sunderson's display.

She never did get to see Helen's stone carved in chocolate. As prophesied, Sunderson had gone bankrupt with the coming of Woolworths. Helen's stone had been introduced to the cemetery quietly and without fanfare. Lucy never entered Woolworths.

Lucy rounded the curve in the cemetery and stopped without thinking. A young woman stood at Ethel's grave. In the twenty years she had visited the cemetery, no one had ever visited Ethel's grave. There had never been a soul in that entire corner of the world. Lucy moved closer, curious. The woman was dressed in white and wore a driving hat. These were certainly not mourning clothes. Nor did she have the air of mourning as she spun her parasol idly in one direction and then the next. Lucy moved closer.

She was brought up short, again, this time by the woman's bearing, her stature, her frame, her hair. They all reminded her of Ethel. Lucy felt a warm flush wash through her body, and stood, beflummoxed. Her body wanted to run to this woman, to embrace her, to forgive her. But her mind spun out the possibilities—was this a ghost? When had she ever seen a ghost wandering the stones? In all of her years, in all of her visits, she hadn't had the slightest inkling of ghosts or hauntings. The woman's bearing was so strikingly Ethel's bearing that Lucy paused—was this Ethel's daughter? But it couldn't have been Ethel's daughter. She'd never had a daughter. She'd never had a son.

Her body continued to draw her toward the woman, as though

there were a deep kindred spirit before her, a spirit who wandered graveyards in general and this particular section in specific. Her mind continued its mystification as her feet took her closer and closer. The parasol spun idly in one direction, then the other. Lucy's feet took her closer. Who was this woman?

She turned, suddenly, quickly enough to startle Lucy, to ready her feet for flying away.

"Oh my," said the young woman. Her hand rose quickly to her mouth. "You startled me."

Lucy apologized, quickly, quietly. The woman didn't look like Ethel at all. Her hair had a similar color, but even the similarity fell by the way once she turned.

"I just adore walking with the dead," she said. She gave a quick smile and an extra spin.

Lucy wasn't quite sure what she meant by that, but she felt a sympathy for the enterprise and communicated that. She studied the woman's eyes. They were the brightest of blues and impenetrable. Everything sparkled on the surface. Lucy asked her where she was from.

"Ohio," the woman said. "I'm on my honeymoon." She held out her hand so that Lucy might admire the diamond on her finger. Lucy noticed the diamond and how delicate the fingers were. She expressed her appreciation for the stone.

"We just stopped for gasoline. We're on an automobile trip," she said. "From Ohio, to Buffalo, where they have the loveliest hotel you ever imagined, to Rochester, Syracuse, and Utica. Now we are headed south to New York City! Can you imagine? New York City!" She recited the rest of their itinerary, a honeymoon that would abandon their automobile in New York City as they boarded a steamer that would take them to Europe and a grand continental tour of the best of all of the places in the world—Paris, Milan, Barcelona.

"We'll be back in time for our firstborn," she concluded.

Lucy asked her if she were expecting. Her sympathies had begun to evaporate.

"If all goes well," the young woman said. "If all goes well."

She paused for several moments, before turning to Ethel and Helen and the rest of the women.

"This is a very liberal place," she gushed. "Imagine, letting the unwed mothers in!"

A horn sounded from the other side of the iron fence. The woman made her quick goodbye. "He just hates it when I'm late. Isn't that adorable?" She ran off, her white skirts fluttering, and her hat nearly left her head with her excitement. The horn sounded again. Lucy could hear the woman cry "Coming!", though she doubted the young man could hear over the sputtering of the motor engine.

It took some time for Lucy to turn her attention to the stones, to Ethel, to Helen. The grass here was long. Longer than across the way. The quietude she sought was hard to come by. She felt the discomfit. She thought she caught the smell of a cigar. Mrs. Harnish's giggle.

．　　．　　．

She left the cemetery just as another engine erupted—a young man began his attack on the grass with a gas-powered grass cutter. At the edge of town, the world quieted considerably. Lucy was able to drop the reins and let the horses follow their noses home. They trudged over the familiar road. Lucy tried to distract herself by listing the chores she had to tend to once she was home. She thought she might pick apples for a pie. She thought she might pick a few extra, either to take to the Westers or to bake an extra pie for them.

The Lamarques' horse pasture was overgrown. She hadn't seen a horse there in five years, it seemed. They had bought an automobile and a tractor and had given up on horses altogether. Lucy missed seeing the animals grazing. She missed the way they lifted their heads at her approach, and how they'd prance alongside the fence, showing off for her mares, their tails held high like roosters. Like bantam roosters.

The pasture had been abandoned. Elms and maples had begun to take over—some were nearly five feet tall already. Even so, they were almost eclipsed by the grasses. She could see two deer's heads as they stretched above the grass to see the horses and wagon. Earlier that spring, she'd thought she'd seen a pair of foxes tumbling and cavorting through the saplings. It was returning to the wild.

On the breeze, the distinct sound of metal on metal. Yellow and Gold plodded on to the sharp bend in the road and barely flicked an ear at the road crew there. They were straightening the road—the sharp loop around the ancient oak was too much for the speed of the automobiles. Two had missed the corner in the recent past. One of the young people had been killed.

One of the men was crouching over a small box. When he heard the sound of Lucy's mares, he rose and ambled over. He reached out and held the mares' reins, forcing Lucy to stop.

"You just made it," he said. "We're closing the road for the rest of the afternoon."

Lucy sat, silent in the wagon. The ancient oak had fallen, away from the road, just where the men had hoped as they had hacked away at its trunk. They had dug at the roots that held what was left of the trunk firmly in place. Lucy shifted slightly in her seat, turning her face to the man, whose chest had begun to swell with the importance of what he was telling her. They were setting the dynamite and would begin blasting within the hour. He released the reins. Yellow and Gold moved on, on their own accord.

The graded road was nicer on the horses' hooves. The grading had crept further and further outside of the town proper—each year, just a little bit more, it seemed, a slow creep that erased the deep imprints of horses' hooves, especially where the road turned to clay. The sound of metal on metal resumed, fading as the horses quickened the pace. Home was on the horizon.

Within the hour, the horses were fed and watered. Hay awaited them in the lower paddock. Lucy's chickens were bedded down for the night. The dogs snuffled and rolled indolently about the lawn. Lucy stood on her porch, feeling summer. Feeling the quiet lack of machinery. She could smell the hay drying in the fields. Melvin would be baling within the next day or two. All was in order.

Lucy stood on her porch. She inhaled. She stretched. She uncoiled her hair. It had grayed, but the change in pigment was difficult to spot. It fell about her shoulders to her waist. Nearby, a wren began chastising a squirrel.

She inhaled, the smell of hay, the smell of summer, the smell of the barn, full and rich, the smell of playing with Ethel in the barn. The corners of her mouth began to turn.

She left the porch and crossed the yard. Her shoes lay in the grass like the strays had, abandoned with tongues hanging out in the early evening heat. She crossed the yard with a skip and a jump, accelerating through the taller grass, picking up speed down the slight slope, down to the creek where the bullfrogs and the snappers lived, Ethel laughing at her side. She stepped into the water, into the muck with a sucking pop, and leapt about, splashing and dancing with her friend.

A distant blast of dynamite.

Lucy giggled and cavorted. Water flew about in every direction. She stomped through the creek. The mud sucked at her feet. Her hair rippled, then, soaked, clung to her back. Lucy was forty-three years old. Lucy was barefoot in the creek. Lucy had a smile that stretched from ear to ear. Lucy was abandoned. Lucy cavorted with wild abandonment.

In the distance, a blast of dynamite.

4

The West Virginian was a surprise. He showed up one day, hat in hands, knocking at her door, asking politely if he might have a glass of water. He waited patiently on the porch while she retrieved a quart jar from the kitchen. She then led him to the pump, where he pumped his own.

He was clean, she thought. His shirt looked new, even if his shoes were nearly worn. After drinking down the jar, his Adam's apple punctuating each swallow, he noticed that she was looking at his shoes. I'm a walker, he explained, and told her that he'd walked nearly everywhere in his fifty-odd years. After his second jar, he told her that he called West Virginia his home, but he hadn't been there in twenty years. He said he'd walked though Kentucky. He'd walked from St. Louis to Oregon and south to San Francisco. He'd walked from Talking Rock, Georgia, and was on his way to Lubec, Maine, to see the largest whirlpool in the Western Hemisphere.

Lucy almost smiles at the memory. Perhaps it was the walking that had surprised her, that he suddenly appeared, unannounced by the rattle and bang of the automobile. Nobody walked anymore, she thought, as he handed her the quart jar. She hadn't seen a body walk past her house in several years. Perhaps it was only the walking that surprised her, that he had no ambition other than to walk. What was in Maine? That wasn't the point, he said. Walking was the point. Walking was the great lost art. He laughed. A solitary art. Walking is best done alone, he told her, otherwise it's dancing. Like dancing, there were all kinds.

He shambled. His left shoulder dropped and brought his head down slightly. His hips settled on his thighs. He heard something as he moved. Lucy could tell from the way his eyes turned inward, he heard something. His right foot scuffed forward. His left foot shuffled behind. His hips kind of rocked in their sockets and everything followed his knees. Lucy almost laughed. It was the most unsightly collection of elbows and joints she'd ever seen.

He strolled, tipping his upper body back back back as he swung from left to right, everything working in harmony. He tipped his hat as he strolled. Strolling is a hat-tipping walk, he said, and smiled, and tipped it again.

He strutted. To the road and back. Shoulders high and stilled. Head slightly cocked. To the road and back, sharp and stiff. There's hundreds of struts, he said, and his body slowed, softening, fluffing into hungry hen. Chickens strut. But, he cautioned, each kind had a strut all to its own, and there was the leghorn jutting forward, legs almost reluctantly darting forward as he turned at the road, his head jerking left, right, left, right right, until it stilled, held steady as though it were a vase filled with flowers and overflowing with water—a French Crevecoeur, regal, unfluffable, unflappable, aristocratic.

He marched, he paced, he sauntered. Up and down the drive he went, with so much energy, so much vim and vinegar that he nearly wore himself out and had to drink another quart of water. One quart shy of a gallon, thought Lucy, who was counting. Harold had told her once that a man would die if he drank a full gallon of water. She worried as she watched this man from West Virginia, who was one quart shy of bursting his bladder and still running through his gaits.

He came to the lope. Dogs lope, he said. Stray dogs have the best lopes around, because they travel. It usually takes four legs to lope, but after miles and miles of practice, he had perfected the two-legged lope. Barnum and Bailey had heard about it and had offered him three hundred dollars a month just to do the two-legged lope for audiences around the world, but he'd turned it down. The lope is a traveling gait, he said. A person goes places at a lope. He went. Down the road, to the west. He was out of sight in less than a minute. Vanished.

Near as she could guess, Harold had vanished at a stride.

Lucy's feet are sore as she stands at the sink. She used to be able to stand for an hour, washing vegetables, washing clothes, washing eggs. No longer. Her feet wear out with each passing moment. Her arches ache, her heels pound with the pressure. The great lost art, she thinks, is standing.

·   ·   ·

There had always been strays. Her father shot twice: once to warn, then to kill. Still, they happened by with a regularity that kept the gun by the kitchen door. After her parents' deaths, Lucy'd put it in their bedroom, in their closet. After Harold left, she'd thought about it, thought about bringing it out again. But it was still in their closet when a mongrel loped through and made a feint for Bo Peep. Lucy was off the porch with a boom of her own. The dog collapsed, as though shot, right where she stood, and rolled her eyes as Lucy set to instructing her about the ways of the world, about chickens and their breeds, about commitment and trespass, about porcupines and horses, about wild abandon and abandonment. Simply translated, all her gesticulations and yammerings, all her finger shakings and lip pursings meant "stay away from the chickens and I'll tolerate your presence." A more refined translation meant that the mongrel found a name and a home. Lucy washed her down and made her a bed of old quilts and let her sleep in the kitchen.

Cinderella doted on Lucy, watching her as she moved through her day, keeping by her side as she walked from the house to the chicken coop to the barn to the fields. She put up such a racket when Lucy left for her Friday trips to town that Lucy eventually allowed her to come along. She would trot by the wagon on the way in. She spent herself racing freely through the cemetery as Lucy walked the paths, visiting the stones, her parents', Helen's, Ethel's, and the others that had become familiar with the passing years. Cinder would exhaust herself in the cemetery, so much that she'd ride in the wagon on the way back to the farm, as lifeless as the sacks of flour or beans.

Cinder also kept other strays at a distance. She'd bolt from the porch and lower her bark to warn them away. For several years, they respected her warnings, respected Cinder herself, and kept their distance. Then came the crisis of '93 and the mysterious disappearances. The Wellers. Bovays. Conklins. Tharretts. All had been hovering on the edge of subsistence and had taken small mortgages. So, the sudden departure of the Crandalls. Rumor had it that they moved to Minnesota, or Wisconsin, where they competed with the Swedes and Norwegians for land. They'd left in June, when the rains failed to come and it became obvious to even the most delusional optimists that, were the deluge itself to materialize before their dusty eyes, they'd never recover their seed money. By July 4th, seventeen families had followed, walking or riding, heading north to Syracuse and then west, along the canal to Rochester and Buffalo, and on to Cleveland, Detroit, and Chicago. West. Some stopped along the way. Others just kept going.

The empty farms were a testament against Homer's bankers, bankers who dangled mortgages in front of Lucy's eyes like cutworms before a chicken. Or so they thought. Spruce the place up, they said. Spruce yourself up. A man likes a well-ordered homestead.

With the abandoned farms were abandoned dogs. They traversed the countryside in packs, flushing rabbits, squirrels, and turkeys and running down deer. The Homer town council voted a bounty, which they quickly rescinded when Wally Coskin brought in what turned out to be the banker's prize terrier. When they tried to arrest Wally for trespassing and theft, there was a near riot in Homer. Some thought Wally hadn't gone far enough, figuring the bounty should have been on Prescott himself, not his dog.

The number of strays quickly decreased as people took them in in belated acts of charity: they became symbols for the seventeen families driven to ruin.

* * *

Twenty-five years later, the strays returned in waves and nearly overran the town. Jim Willickson, who had bought the Crandall farm for the pittance of the mortgage that was due, worked the farm for more than twenty years before giving in to the soil: it was simply good for nothing but hay. Try as he might, Willickson couldn't get anything else to take. The meager production of corn or potatoes bought him nothing but misery. He raised three sons, who were little better than the potatoes they ate, saw them off the farm, and promptly sold the place to two fast talkers from New England. Willickson and Daisy, his wife, left for California. Lucy wasn't sorry to see them go. Daisy would call on her in the middle of the day, when she was busy with canning or pickling, and want to chat for an hour about nothing. She expected Lucy to make tea. She expected Lucy to remove her apron when she chatted and to sit in the parlor. She would bring men by, "eligible" men she called them. The last thing Daisy said to Lucy was to keep her hair combed. Both New Englanders were "eligible" and she wouldn't want to scare them off with untended tresses.

Lucy wasn't sorry to see the Willicksons go until Haffolk and Roone began building. Suddenly Daisy's intrusions seemed a bit more bearable, if not preferable. They talked fast and funny. Lucy wasn't sure if they were poking fun at her expense when they laughed. They laughed loud and open-mouthed. Lucy decided she didn't like seeing their teeth like that. She never did get their first names.

Worse, what they built was a fledgling chicken hatchery. It was paid for, in part, by the United States Army, so they could supply the troops with eggs. It was 1917. The racket they raised when they set to building their first long, low chicken house was greater than the front lines of the Great War itself. They hammered twenty-four hours a day. The noise was so great with the hammering and the steam engine that Lucy's chickens didn't lay for three weeks. She thought they were egg bound and would have called the veterinarian if he hadn't been supervising the construction.

The steam engine dredged the creek and rerouted much of its flow. For a week, there was no water at all in the creek bed that ran through Lucy's land. Then, it came roaring through—brown and thick and sometimes roiling, a chicken foot or head bubbling to the surface.

Lucy nearly screamed with the horror of it.

The stray dogs found the creek. They came to it as to a spa and lapped up the broth-like elixir. They gamboled through her fields. They lounged on the banks. When they ran through her yard, catching Mina Loy and savaging her, more for sport than for feeding their hunger, Lucy fairly flew out of her kitchen. The dogs scrambled. Her chickens burst up in an array of red and gold.

That night, as the sun set over the hatchery, Lucy entered her parents' bedroom for the first time in years. She found her father's shotgun in the closet.

• • •

Lucy couldn't look out her kitchen window without seeing the hatchery. In 1923, they added another long, low building, another summer ruined with shouts and pounding. In 1928, a third. They lobbied for a spur track to hook up to the main rail line. They sold chicks all over the northern states and maintained a fleet of trucks that raised the dust on the road as they roared past.

What went on inside the hatchery was unnatural. Or so Lucy heard. She really didn't want to know. To begin, they hired a chicken sexer.

A chicken sexer.

The town bustled over that. Lucy bustled over that. She threw a hitch into her bustle when she learned just what a chicken sexer did. She shuddered each time the thought arose, bringing with it the stale taste of bile, until she could stand it no more. On one of her Fridays, she marched in to Kesling's and ordered shutters for her kitchen window. Anything to stop the madness.

．　　．　　．

Rising on the breeze, feathers, the joy of Haffolk and Roone's Austrolorps feasting merrily on her Araucanas. She saw them fluttering. She heard them calling to her, clearly, as clearly as if she were there. As clearly as if she were in hell itself. Lucy closed her eyes, full-body pause—her hand stilled in midair, fingers poised, her breath in midway between inhale and ex, her lungs, her windpipe, her nostrils at once filled and not filled with the passage of air. The breeze died. The merry sounds fell with it. But their effects lingered in the front room of the farmhouse. Lucy sat, quiet, eyes slowly opening in the dimmed light of the room.

She had slowly begun to move into this room, a room unused for twenty-five years, a cold room, away from the stove, facing the north, facing the road, shaded further by the porch and its overhang. She had slowly begun to move into this room with the coming of the factory.

She appreciated the view of the road, appreciated her view of the man from West Virginia as he kicked up the dust. Years before, she had taken such a view from the porch, of Harold as he came to court. She wasn't "out" now, hidden behind the glass, hidden behind the curtains, in the shade of the overhang, invisible to the road.

Her view, now, was the same as it had always been. It was cut off to the west by the hedgerow of honeysuckle, larger now, large enough for a bear to hide in. The hedgerow was sickeningly sweet at times, thicker than pungent, so thick that the bees it drew walked the air to its flowers. To the west, the old, old field, hidden by the honeysuckle. It was last worked before she was born and was used up then, the thin layer of dirt, hardly soil, barely covered the enormous rock bed underneath.

The field was the same from year to year, Queen Anne's lace flowers in the middle summer, with the black-eyed Susans and other tall grasses. By late summer, they were husks, burned out from lack of water. To the north, across the road, the hayfield. To the east, at least as far as she could see from her window—oaks. Ageless oaks growing older. They were older than her father, she knew. Whether the road came before the oaks, or the oaks before the road, she had no idea. She wondered, idly, about the two dozen that lined her land, fronting the barn and the fields to the east.

Her surprise was new. She sat, eyes reacquainting themselves to the darkened room, lungs filling with air, her hands returning to their sewing.

Her surprise was new. On the road, on foot, appearing suddenly but without sudden gestures—the man from West Virginia. He walked without sound, if such things were possible she found herself thinking, or walked under the sound of the factory, or with his shuffles and scuffs whisked away on the breeze.

Harold had appeared in such a way, but wholly without surprise. His whistling lips, his jaunty walk, his dancing feet, could be heard for half a mile, setting Lucy into an attenuated quiver, full-body paroxysm of trembles, twitches, and other bits of spasms. She didn't know why she had reacted so. She didn't know why she would drop a stitch here, add one there, prick herself with her needle, the threads darting about the material that lay in her lap until she was sewn to her own quilt, a second skin. So, Harold had appeared, but wholly without surprise, as though his presence, his absence on the horizon was entirely natural, expected. Nor had there been any surprise at the peculiar conjunction of his appearance, whistling, dancing, twirling, and the activity in which she had been engaged: filling her hope chest with the linens, bed sheets, tablecloths, and quilts that would see a young couple through their first decade and beyond. This conjunction had seemed entirely natural, even as she'd trembled at the sound of his whistle, twitched with his jaunty walk, and spasmed with his dancing feet.

Her surprise was multiplied. The man from West Virginia's sudden appearance caught her unaware, like the passing shadow of a large bird, momentarily leaving her absolutely still. What surprised her more, however, was her own self. With his appearance, her head tilted inexplicably and slightly to the right. She felt the rarified air passing through her left nostril and into her left lung. She registered the faintest, ever-so-faint, prickle of skin along the left side of her neck, up, into the back of her head. Goose bumps, Ethel would have said. Chicken shit, Harold would have replied.

With that, her surprise nearly knocked her out of her chair. Her body, its tilt, its conforming to the air, its prickling skin, told her for half a moment that it was Harold, this, even as she knew, even as her body knew, it was not.

Her surprise was her body, and what it told her.

She watched him pass.

She dismissed her surprise.

She dismissed her body.

She dismissed everything she knew and returned to her sewing.

Her mother's sewing club had met once a month in this room. She couldn't remember ever seeing a man in it. The sewing club had regaled Lucy with their trip, years and years before, to Ithaca, to a woman's rights convention. They'd stayed three days and had heard Miss Anthony and Miss Filkins talk about the rights and the roles of women after the war. Lucy had been to Ithaca, to The People's Store. It had placed an ad in the Homer *Ode* that boasted

Eggs Taken In Trade. Lucy had taken her eggs, eggs that were already ruined from the shaking on the roads. The clerk had thought there was something wrong with them because they were blue. She'd wanted a good pair of shoes for the field, but all they would trade for were silk underwear and nightdresses. She'd chosen Nile green; it stood out from the flesh, stood out from the peach, from the tan, from the white, colors that faded into the world.

She was sewing nothing so fancy as that. She was sewing a summer shawl. A reddish orange summer shawl. The color of those damn chickens of yours, Josh Kesling had said when she bought the lightly woven fabric shot with slubbed, metallic thread. It was the color of sunsets, she'd thought when she'd bought it. She'd noticed that the weave caught the light in one direction but not from others. She'd come up with a silly idea, something that would take time, more time than she'd cared to give, but it was her idea: to cut the fabric and sew it back together with the weave in each section facing a different way. The light would ripple across it, she'd thought.

She sat in the light of the window, facing the road, slowly running the needle through the fabric in the tiniest of stitches. The constant shifting and turning reminded her of Harold. She hadn't thought about him for years. Not consciously. She hadn't wanted to. Finding him working his way through her brain had given her pause. He had been a foolish boy, that much was certain. He had been a mere twenty years old, whistling down the road with his head full of dreams. She surprised herself with the thoughts that trickled through her own head. It had never been love, she realized. Nor was she sure she'd even liked him, though she was sure she had a certain fondness for that abbreviated year. No, she had simply marveled at a boy. She nearly dropped a stitch with the thought, and smiled at herself. She hoped that he had panned for gold in Alaska, that he had ridden the freights across the country, that he had sailed in the South Seas. She shifted her chair to better catch the light and bent into her next stitch.

Her chair continued to shift with the passing weeks. It moved closer and closer to the window, arguably for the better light it cast on her sewing. With the chair, her body shifted in its orientation. At the beginning of the summer, she had been angled slightly to the west, to have the light come better over her right shoulder as she stitched. Two months later, she found herself full-facing the glass; the northern light asked her to lean forward over her work, and, by virtue of such a tilt, made her look for all the world like a hen about to peck at something. Her new orientation, her new tilt gave her a more panoramic view of the road and its dust.

She was surprised at the number of times the man from West Virginia crossed her view. At first, she hardly noticed the shambles, the struts, the stuttered lopes as he made his way along the road. Her body noticed, however, and turned her more and more toward the glass. When her mind finally caught on, she trembled. What was she thinking? Her fingers sped along the fabric. Idle hands permitted such thoughts. She left her sewing and doused her hands in the sink, washing a half dozen eggs along the way.

. . .

One Friday in late August, she returned from town with two hundred seedlings. The weather was warm, humid, the worst of the year. But the seedlings couldn't wait for the weather, and she spent the better part of Saturday digging small holes. About midday she took a break. The seedlings themselves were beginning to turn brown. Matthew Kripps, she thought, should have known better than to dig them so early. Kripps, four years her junior. Kripps, who had pulled her hair when she was ten. Kripps, who threw apples at horses as they passed. Kripps, who never did learn to add or count to a hundred. Kripps, who couldn't tell the difference between a brown seedling and a green.

Lucy drew another bucket and soaked the seedlings, leaving them in the shade while she walked the yard to the hedgerow and continued to dig the small holes. It was warm. Considerably warm. By all counts, Kripps should never have sold her the seedlings so late in the summer. Later, maybe, or so much earlier. But not so that they had to be planted in the high heat of summer. It was a terrible time to be planting, she thought.

"Terrible time to be planting."

She would have jumped through the clouds with surprise had she not heard the soft crunch of his shoes across the dried lawn and seen the birds in the hedgerow flitting away with his approach. As it was, she nearly jumped through the clouds with the surprising echo, her own thoughts tangible, walking with the bees on the ever-thickening air. She stood, suspecting the West Virginian, for the sound of his feet was different from the sound of any other feet she'd ever heard. The voice itself was unexpected, or, rather, unfamiliar. The faintest traces of another land, southern but not the South, both drawn and pinched at one and the same time. So, her own thoughts, reflected as if in a fun house at the fair, came to her distorted, drawn, and pinched.

"But I can see a considerable need," he said, completing her unthought premise. He stood beside her, the two of them looking west over the chicken factory.

She turned toward him, confirming the connection between voice and speaker.

"Wallace Tromble," he said, introducing himself.

Lucy took his outstretched hand.

"Lucy Delano," she replied.

"Pleased, to be sure," he said, and, pausing to look at the factory, "Terrible sight, indeed." She had little time to respond, barely a moment to blink, before he had the shovel in his hand, completing the hole she'd begun, moving quickly on to the next. She had little opportunity to respond, for he was talking all the while, telling her a story about a time when he'd come upon a horribly ugly sight, a scar upon the world, a tragedy of Homeric proportions. Lucy squeezed a thought in edgewise, and a sidereal glance to see if he was having fun with the town. He wasn't, and named the rail yards at Chicago, as a point of fact. From those atrocities of timber and steel, he had gone to get a meal at the local mission, where he had learned from the Matrons of the Publick Eye, that there was work beautifying Chicago from the blight of the industrialists. He'd worked. He'd beautified the city with shovel and pick, with shrubs and trees, and as he'd shoveled and picked, he'd noted that the biggest contributors to the beautification project were the wives of the industrialists.

"The entire business made me a Wobbly," he said. She squeezed in another sideways glance, blinked, and was about to comment, but he was already admiring her plan.

"Pity it takes pines so long to grow," he said. He noticed the seedlings when he approached, barely a foot tall. "Of course some folks have the time." He didn't mean her. He meant Teddy Roosevelt. He meant how he'd nearly broken his back working for Roosevelt's conservation program, a program with "its vision for future generations." He liked that, and regaled her with descriptions of future generations where everyone wore Teddy Roosevelt glasses. . . .

Lucy drifted off as Wallace spun his story, drifted to the pump where she drew another bucket and poured it on the seedlings, drifted into her own thoughts, to the past. Her father should have worn glasses, of this she was certain. It might have helped with the headaches he'd had. She thought, briefly, about placing a pair on his grave. But Wallace yelped, having nearly put the shovel through his foot as he dug, and she turned to the hedgerow, to the road, to the man from West Virginia, to the future.

•   •   •

The seedlings have finally taken hold, she thinks, as she stands at her sink. For two years, they spent their energy underground, leaving the needles to fend for themselves. But now, five years later, the leader and branches have taken off, growing as much as a foot a year. They are still spindly, transparent. Lucy dips an egg in the soapy water. Kripps. He'd died last year, suddenly, but it hadn't surprised anyone. "Struck down as if by lightning, this oak of a man will be sorely missed," opined the *Ode*. "He'd taken shelter under a massive hickory planted by his grandfather, manning the helm, soaked by a raging storm," then she'd had to stop reading. She'd dropped the paper to the floor as she'd nearly choked on her own laughter.

Wallace, who was full of stories, told her about a farmer down in Pennsylvania who'd suffered nine visits from chicken thieves. No matter what he did, the thieves managed to steal a chicken or three. This farmer had set dogs out on the prowl without luck. He'd let his bull range free in the night. He'd gone so far as to sleep in the coop, shotgun in hand, and slept he had as the thieves slipped four hens from under his head! Finally, this poor sap had decided to put up an electric burglar alarm. The first night, the alarm set to wailing, and had him leaping out of the bed thinking all the world had ended. It had, for two of his hens who had been bold enough to peck at the copper wire as the moon shone, glinted, off it. He'd found them dead, their beaks clamped around the bar so tight he couldn't remove them. As he'd fussed and fussed, with the chickens and the copper, he'd managed to electrocute himself with enough charge to blow the line all the way in to the town. Wallace had laughed when he told the story.

Lucy had tried to laugh, but all she could see were those unsuspecting hens drawn to the copper.

She'd had her own thieves, but she'd never thought them funny. When he'd asked, she'd told Wallace of the summer of '93, when she'd heard a rustling in her hen house in the small hours.

She'd gone out, clutching a shovel, her father's shotgun forgotten at the time, gone out noisily, hoping to scare the animal away. The rustling had continued as she approached, and so, without thinking much one way or the other, she'd lifted the shovel and smacked the side of the coop. That had caught the attention of the intruder, and he'd yelped, rolled out the door and away, running for all he was worth on two legs, ducking low, certain, no doubt, that a shotgun blast would be right behind. Lucy had gone back to bed. In the morning, she'd found seven new chickens, Hamburgs from the looks of them.

Wallace had laughed long at that, pausing in his whitewashing of the barn, dripping paint all over himself, all over the ground for her hens to later peck at as though the splattered gobs were grubs.

Lucy recalls those seven chicken. They were black and white, spangled, blue-legged, smallish, free ranging, and, no doubt, direct descendants from those few birds that survived that brutal first winter in New Amsterdam. Dorkings were also black and white, though of a different time with their heavy wattles and extra toes. When Homerites said that the Dorkings were from Rome, they meant that venerable and ancient time, not the town of Rome some miles up the road. Several years later, Orpingtons were all the rage. With their golden buffery and English pedigree, they preened about the farmsteads as if they were newly landed gentry and deserving of every title no matter how slight. Lucy's Araucanas, however, were Homer's *first* golden layers. They were positively primal in their scratchings and puffery, in their hems and caws, as if they had come from the first jungle, the jungle preceding all jungles, predated only by the most ancient of all gardens.

She finds her reverie broken by Wallace's five-year-old laughter, and she is wrenched from that garden, from her first chickens, from Victoria, Catherine, Elizabeth, Winifred, Gwendolyn, and Maude and their capers.

Although he'd admired her Araucanas, Wallace had thought Australorps the best chickens for laying. Australian Orpingtons, he'd said. Imagine importing a chicken from Australia! He had worked the shovel as he'd marveled at the thought, the dirt, loam, turning, revealing a host of night crawlers. Lucy could almost imagine a copper wire as she'd watched the worms, and had sat, quickly, as if stung.

She sets her jaw. Australorps were never great layers. Australorps were meat birds. Australorps were the pride and joy of the New Englanders next door and had won blue ribbons at the county fair. Wallace's laugh again. Mrs. Harnish's giggle. The close smell of cigars and sweat mixed with their laughter. Lucy sets her jaw.

• • •

Melvin makes the turn and crosses her field of vision. The Westers had seen something in Wallace, enough to send Melvin by with a bit of torn newspaper one day.

Dancing
The Hanging Gardens
Weds and Sat Evenings
Music by Hank Fullerton, Homer's Popular Dance Orchestra.
Good parking for cars.
Gentlemen $1.00 Ladies Free.
Refreshments.
Dancing 9–1.

He'd handed it to her with the announcement that his parents were thinking of taking a spin that Saturday night to see how good the parking really was. She knew what they were thinking, but found herself at a complete loss.

• • •

She was at a complete loss for words. Wallace read her thoughts on Thursday, dipped his head to one side, and said he'd be flattered. He kicked up a heel. Dancing. Second-best thing to walking, and he winked. She thought there was a joke in the wink, but she wasn't sure.

She was frozen, speechless, in the backseat of the Westers' Ford, wedged between Wallace and Melvin, terrified at the speed with which they flew. She could see the speedometer from where she sat—forty miles per hour! She was too terrified to confess that she'd never ridden in an automobile before. Trees, fence posts, drives emerged suddenly in the headlights and disappeared just as quickly. A rabbit froze by the side of the road as they roared along. Melvin and Wallace tried to sing something and struggled through several verses before giving up.

The Hanging Gardens overwhelmed her, filling her senses and stealing her voice. Although it was within sight of the cemetery, she'd never before been so close, nor taken much notice. All the automobiles! She hadn't imagined there could be so many. They lined the swooping U-shaped drive and revealed their luster with the passing headlights. She thought she caught glimpses of couples standing, smoking, between the black and shimmering machines, but the building itself, with its seven columns rising skyward, lit from below with spotlights, quickly filled her attention. The entrance led to a grand ballroom. Already at this early hour, twenty or more couples swirled and swooped over the marbled floor. Before they could take it all in, Melvin pulled them all to the side, to the greenhouse—two stories tall and filled with trees, bushes, and plants that hung from the ceiling. This was what gave the building its name. The humidity inside the glass walls was high, but it held the rich sweet smells of the flowers and the leaves and the soil—she could smell the soil, too, a dark rotting smell that felt strangely alive. Wallace kicked up his heels and traced something in the glass, but the water ran and ruined it before she could see. She could barely keep her air. She drew it in well enough, but it stayed in her throat, never making it to her lungs. It made her feel top-heavy, lightheaded.

She could not escape her discomfort.

On the dance floor, couples swirled and swooped. A shiny, sparkling ball twirled overhead, sending spatters of light over everyone and everything. Young men gathered around the bar and laughed long, honking laughs. Young women twittered along the wall.

She could not escape her discomfort.

On the drive home, she closed her eyes. As much as that helped her avoid the tunnel vision of the headlights and the sudden emergence of rabbits and trees and deer, the bumps and turns made her slightly nauseous and she was more than relieved when the headlights played across the front of her house and the automobile came, at last, to rest. She was even more relieved to hear its engine fade into the night.

•   •   •

The following Wednesday, she read the *Ode* in the hour before darkness fell. As she drifted from one page to the next, she was struck by the number of references to automobiles—almost as though the paper were dedicated to the machines. There were the advertisements, too many to count. (Someday you'll own two cars, why wait? one asked. Lucy doubted she would ever ride in one again.) There was the notice that Albert Robinson had been discharged on a technicality. He had been charged with speeding—driving a reckless thirty-four miles per hour through the village—but the sign that indicated the limit was thirty miles per hour had been taken down. Albert claimed to have been going twenty-two. Lucy wondered how fast one could walk.

She was shocked by the article that reported 3412 cars had passed through the village of Homer on Saturday between 7 A.M.

and 7 P.M. There had been an additional 44 trucks and 6 motorcycles. The number was incomprehensible to her—that there could be so many automobiles was beyond belief, that they were all out and about was beyond comprehension. Surely this couldn't have counted their drive to the Hanging Gardens, for that had happened later. How could it have not? And all of the other cars in the parking lot? Uncounted! That there could be so much movement, so much motion, was itself beyond anything she could imagine.

The dance floor at the Hanging Gardens had been more than enough movement for her. The bodies flying about, their feet hopping and sliding across the floor. Wallace was a better walker than he was a dancer. He stepped on her feet and kicked her once so hard that she doubled over with the suddenness of it. Of course it was her fault, because she couldn't master the art of getting out of the way—that's what she decided as she watched the women move—they spent all of their energy moving out of the way of their partners, who quickly moved into the spot they'd just vacated. Lucy was better at standing than dancing, she thought. It was too difficult to get out of the way, to worry that someone else wanted to be where she was.

Her eyes fell on a frightening story: A young girl had leapt from a moving automobile and was knocked unconscious. It grew more horrible with each line. The girl had been visiting Homer and had gone with a young man to the Hanging Gardens on Saturday evening. Lucy worried that she'd seen the young girl, but there was not enough description to tell. She'd danced through the night. The young man who had driven her to the dance had fallen asleep in his car. She hadn't seen him when she left, and had been walking home when another young man pulled up and informed her that her mother was sick. She got in. Lucy could barely read on. Her mother had never been sick. The young man had been following her through the night. Lucy shuddered as she imagined the poor girl, leaping from the car. The shudder brought an early memory of Josh Kesling driving up and down her road, tearing the macadam right out of the ground with his rubber tires. Mrs. Harnish's giggle and the smell of cigars. Wallace's silly attempt at a kiss. The *Ode* slid to the floor. Her feet stilled, amidst the paper.

• • •

The following Saturday, Wallace sat on her porch, sipping a glass of water. It had a bit of lemon crushed in it, in the fashion of the water served at the Hanging Gardens the previous Saturday. Wallace brought the lemon. He wore his "sitting clothes" as he called them, different from his walking clothes. Different from his working clothes. The bucket of whitewash remained in the shed, with the brush and ladder.

He sipped on his glass of water.

The sun beat down. After a cool morning, the temperatures had risen quickly.

His hand drifted across the short space between the chairs and came to a rest on hers.

Lucy noticed the difference. His hand on hers, the assuredness with which it landed, the assuredness with which his forefinger rose and fell, tapping a slow waltz or shamble or shuffle, made her feel uneasy, as though she were still in the Westers' automobile. Her uneasiness was all the more disconcerting for disturbing the comfort of her own front porch.

Lucy noticed the difference in Wallace's bearing. So different from the fumbled kiss he'd tried to deliver after the dance, on this same porch, as she was slipping through the door, the Westers having just dropped them off with heady "good-byes." Wallace had declined a ride home, poohpawing the easy transportation. A few dances hadn't taken the walk out of his feet, he'd said, while Lucy gained the porch. His feet had taken the steps quickly as she opened the door. His lips had not been so agile, not been so coordinated. Once inside, she'd not known what to think. He'd nearly skipped down the road, whistling one of Fullerton's songs. She had been careful to throw the lock on the door before she walked up the stairs to her bed.

His hand came to rest on hers. She tried not to look at it, tried to look at the field across the road, at the geese as they milled, pausing to collect themselves for their great migration south.

"Rats with wings," said Wallace. Sipping.

The description caught her by surprise and momentarily distracted her from the weight of his hand on hers. She slowly became aware that her heart was pounding. She thought about Harold and closed her eyes in a whispered farewell. Her heart slowed. The touch, the weight, the rising and falling of his finger began to feel comfortable, natural, welcome. The muscles that surrounded her mouth began to relax. The whitewashing could wait. Her hens began drifting to the front of the house, pecking at the ground in front of them. They came on in ones and threes, Justine, then Tug and Ella-child and Gloria. Princess. Then Plain Jane. They scuttled ahead and stopped, scuttled and stopped. Plain Jane rose on flapping wings, a furious flurry.

Wallace began humming a Fullerton tune, a waltz.

Lucy almost smiled at her hens, how they almost moved in concert with the sweeping three-beat phrases, almost. Each movement, however, lagged, stuttered, or dragged, emphasized the almost. She almost sighed. She almost smiled.

She shifted slightly in her chair, and turned her hand palm up under his. Her fingers curled, and his curled in turn, their hands coming into a full embrace on the arm of her chair. The sun was warm. The whitewashing could wait.

Rascal came strutting around the corner, his own four-beat step running counter to the hens. His colors were bold against the fading landscape. Rascal was bold against the fall landscape. Her hens warbled and cooed softly as they pecked. Wallace was watching a solitary cloud slowly disintegrating in the sky. His hand pressed against hers. Lucy nearly closed her eyes.

Rascal hurried his four-beat step, darting at Plain Jane, who protested with a squawking flutter, bursting from the ground, sending the rest of the hens upward with sudden beats of their wings. Wallace's hand withdrew just as suddenly, without warning. He was on his feet, stepping off the porch before the hens landed.

Her own hand felt the abandonment only for a moment before it was swept into motion. Lucy rose just as suddenly, without warning, instinctively, away from Wallace and the yard, to the kitchen door, to her father's shotgun.

She unloaded, without thinking, just as Wallace had snapped the rooster's neck, the explosion drowning out his own exclamation "Roosters complicate the flock," drowning out his admonishment that she should have killed the rooster out of the egg.

Wallace was off, down the road in a scuffling of feet heretofore unnamed, his hands clutching his buttocks, his face bearing a deep and uncomprehending wound, but the second blast kept him from turning and revealing it to Lucy. The geese in the field across the road rose, hundreds of startled, honking geese taking wing, taking flight, taking the color out of the sky.

Lucy was reloading, filling the chamber with cracked corn, firing again and again, long after Wallace was out of sight, firing to the west, firing at Haffolk, at Roone, at the factory. Each blast kicked against her shoulder, knocking her against the porch, knocking her off her feet, concussive blasts that carried over the fields and that raised the flock again and again, that brought the Westers sputtering up in their automobile. Rascal lay lifeless in the yard, feathers dancing with the breeze.

• • •

The eggs are clean and damp and sit on a towel next to the sink. Lucy dries her hands. A small pack of dogs runs the field. She can see them through the glass, wild dogs, ghost dogs. Her shotgun leans, forgotten, in the pantry closet. Her eggs are blue, soft, and luminous. These are the eggs that would have won her a blue ribbon at the state fair. These are the eggs that fill her egg basket so perfectly, one by one, without the faintest sound of shell against shell. The basket weighs nothing on her arm. Her shawl catches the light and shimmers, a thousand reflections in a thousand directions. She hears the ghost dogs baying as she walks with her basket full of sky.

The road to Homer is smooth. Automobiles sputter past on her way in.

The road home is smoother. The road home is always smoother without the sounds of egg shells clacking together.

Lucy steps from the kitchen, around the house, to the south, away from the road, away from the factory. She clucks and caws as she moves and she clutches her egg basket. The stain is gone, faded with the years. She squats and spreads her dress such that it forms a near perfect circle about her. She slowly removes the pins from her hair and it cascades, a gray tumbling against her dress, and so lost in her dreams, she forgets why it is so important, forgets why she curves her neck just so, tilts her head, just so, and calls to her chickens in a lilting, spiraling call: Here Josephine. Here Hester. Here Hanna Hoes. Here Jacqueline. Here Mary Ellen. Here Nelly. Here Abigail Childress. Here Sarah. Her attitude is compelling, and the sound of her voice flies to the sun and brings it to rise over the trees, over the trees that hide Homer. She clucks and caws on this dawning Saturday, having forgotten everything but their names. Here Plain Jane. Here Weewaw. Here Jaunty Girl. Here Racer. On they come, Victoria becoming Catherine becoming Elizabeth becoming Winifred becoming Maude. A dizzying becoming. On they come, fluffing and preening, their heads cocked to the left, to the right, they flock about her and scratch at the grass, they scratch at her dress, hungry for grubs, hungry for choice morsels, and, so claim their rightful place in the world.

Epilogue

The skunks began to arrive in Homer, N.Y. They came along the river with their noses pointed high. They came across the fields, nuzzling their way through the long grasses. They followed the roads and the railroad tracks and the hedgerows, bustling and snuffling in with a five-beat trundle all of their own. At first, they were spotted only at night, and only then, by chance. Then they began to be seen at dawn, at dusk, as they grew bolder and bolder, stalking the streets, scrumbling their way through the gardens, shuffling from yard to yard. They moved with the calm assurance of hunting animals, led by their noses, drawn by the faintest whiffs of rot. Their tails, striped and raised—some mostly black, some frosted with white, some double striped, some sporting three or four or five white trails of varying widths against a sheen of black—their tails danced behind them. They scuttled about, alone. They tumbled in groups of two, three, ten, a score, and more. They filled the streets with their snuffles and their squealing chatter.

The town grew quiet. The town grew quieter, nearly silent, afraid to slam a door, to call to a child, to bang a pot, or to sneeze for fear of a scented response. The town grew still with the fear that a black and white surprise might be lurking in the bushes outside their doors or sleeping beneath their windows. They scuffled in the flowerbeds as they dug and dug for the blue bulbs in the dirt. Their soft paddings echoed through the streets. The jaunty swish of tails sounded thunderous in the quietude.

They met in the cemetery, under a blazing sun, where they routed and snuffled amidst the headstones.

A small convocation snorted and pawed around Grambly's family plot. Two skunks burrowed into the grass at the foot of Heywood's stone, which towered above them. Haskins' mausoleum was a fortress; they tunneled under. They savaged the graves of Mumsford, Mackinaw, and Walker. They lolled over the Blighs, the Harmons, the Finks. They twittered and cavorted amidst the dead. They tumbled and rolled among the Effings, the Turners, the Cobs. The Anfalls cursed their distinctive noses and held their eternal breaths.

A telephone rang.

Darkness descended.

A stray dog loped through.

Darkness deepened, blotting out the moon and stars.

With the morning, the skunks disappeared. One or two lingered with the dawn before ambling off through the streets and out of town with their tails alive and dancing. In their wake, they left behind hundreds upon hundreds of bits of sky—tiny blue shards—and the god-awful stench that buried the living and woke the dead.